A Second Chance

A Second Chance

a novel

Felicia Mihali

Cover design: Debbie Geltner

Cover image: Hans Hoffmann (German, about 1530 - 1591/1592), Flowers and Beetles, 1582, Gouache with white chalk over black chalk on vellum, 32.1 x 38.7 cm (12 5/8 x 15 1/4 in.), The J. Paul Getty Museum, Los Angeles

Book design and typesetting: WildElement.ca

Author photo: Martine Doyon

Library and Archives Canada Cataloguing in Publication

Mihali, Felicia, 1967-, author
     A second chance / Felicia Mihali.

Issued in print and electronic formats.

ISBN 978-1-927535-41-7 (pbk.).--ISBN 978-1-927535-44-8 (epub).--
ISBN 978-1-927535-45-5 (mobi).--ISBN 978-1-927535-46-2 (pdf)
     I. Title.
PS8576.I295343S42 2014   C813'.6   C2013-907839-8
                                                 C2013-907840-1

Printed and bound in Canada by Marquis Book Printing.

Legal Deposit, National Library and Archives Canada
et Dépôt légal, Bibliothèque et archives nationales du Québec.

Linda Leith Publishing acknowledges the support of the Canada Council for the Arts and of SODEC.

Linda Leith Publishing
P.O. Box 322, Station Victoria
Westmount, Quebec H3Z 2V8 Canada
www.lindaleith.com

At seven o'clock, I get out of bed and dress warmly. The forecast is twenty below. I would like to stay in bed a bit longer, but I've managed to spoil Ana's dog Billy, in spite of all Ana's warnings. As soon as he wakes up, Billy starts racing between the stairs and the door of our bedroom. Ana has told me he can hold on until nine o'clock, but this is never the case when he stays with us. At seven, I have to take him out.

Adam stares at me, waiting for some explanation, but I'm in no mood to talk. I often get up early, but not to go outside. On weekends I like to read in bed, and it irks me to have to pull on snow pants and mittens at such an early hour. There are six more days until Ana gets back on Christmas Eve.

I let Adam guess my state of mind. Billy gets up on his hind legs at the side of the bed and licks his hand.

Adam's questioning eyes follow me as I leave the bedroom: what should he do? Should he get up, too?

Yet I continue the torture. I leave the house without saying anything.

It's so difficult to walk a male dog, especially a schnauzer that sweeps up so much trash in its long beard. Billy susses out the social scene through the urine spots he sniffs intensely and at length. He's looking for female scents. In the summer, when I look after my friend Carmen's dog, Sake, things are a lot easier. Over the years I have gotten used to the unruly little Shi Tzu who jumps on everything

1

that moves – children, cars, cyclists. Billy is as serious as an old sage. He pays no attention to pedestrians; he's too busy dashing from one sidewalk to the other but, unlike Sake, he never goes up driveways.

Billy has a crush on winter car shelters. He lives in Roxboro, which doesn't allow its citizens to set up those huge white tents over their driveways. Perhaps it's because they're new to him that the shelters excite him. He pees a few drops at almost every one we pass. Fine by me; at this time of the day there's no one at the window to glare at us.

When we're back home, Billy keeps still as I towel down his paws. His fur and beard are sodden, and it takes a while to dry them. Because of his bushy eyebrows, I can never make eye contact with him and can only guess his feelings when he realizes I'm getting ready to walk him. That's the only time he has the sparkle of youth: he jumps, he barks, he rolls on the rug. The rest of the time, he's as still as a sphinx. Unlike Sake, he sleeps all day long when he stays here. I imagine he's a bit depressed until he gets used to us.

Ever since my daughter Sara moved in with Ana's son, Michael, Billy has spent some part of the holidays at our place. We're the only ones who stay in town. We always have Sara and Michael over on Christmas Eve, but on New Year's Eve, we watch TV, just the two of us.

This used to make us feel guilty. While everyone else we know is eating, drinking, kissing, and wishing one another Happy New Year, we were lolling around in our pyjamas. Now, I'm finally OK with spending the holidays at home. My excuse for not joining our friends in the country is Adam's condition.

He's still in bed when I get home. He figured it was too early to get dressed. His instinct told him to wait a bit longer, at least long enough for the living room to warm up, for we turn the thermostat down overnight. Does he know it's Saturday morning and I'm on vacation?

"You should have put the kettle on," I tell him when I've finished drying Billy.

He gets out of bed as fast as possible, puts on his slippers, and goes straight to the kitchen.

"Get dressed first." I yell to him from downstairs where I'm hanging up my coat. "There's no rush."

He goes back into the bedroom without saying a word and turns his face to the wall to take off his pyjama pants and put on his underwear. Adam has learned not to keep his underwear on in bed, as it's too warm under the duvet.

The house smells good because of the fir tree. This year the kids insisted we have a real one, as tall as the ceiling, and they came over to help me decorate it. They asked me to open boxes in the garage with stuff I hadn't touched in years. They probably thought their dad would notice it. The fact that he was playing with a finger-sized plastic Indian gave them some hope. Sara encouraged him to hang it up on the tree. She even showed him a spot on a lower branch to make it easier for him. Adam hung the ornament shyly, then refused to touch any other decoration.

He helped half-heartedly until the moment Sara asked for his good hand. It's a tradition in our family for us to hold hands when we put the golden star on top of the tree. Adam smiled politely and tried to get out of it. I've avoided telling the kids that he dislikes being touched on either the good arm or the bad one. That evening, for the children, he was trying to do what was asked of him, but his eyes were looking at me desperately. He was begging to be rescued, but I hesitated to do so in front of the kids.

Adam keeps his body to himself, revealing it only in the privacy of the bedroom. He has almost never touched me in public in all the years we've been together. When he feels like stroking my hand during some boring dinner party, he just passes me the salt or the pepper as a way of showing that he loves me.

Physical contact with anyone other than me fills him with terror. His doctor is a woman, and an appointment with her almost makes him cry. During his monthly hospital check-ups, I chat with her in French, and Adam stalls for time behind the screen where he is undressing. He delays as long as he can before telling me, in Romanian, that he's ready. Then I leave the doctor's office quickly to avoid the painful moment when his eyes fill with tears and he has to surrender himself to her touching, pinching, listening.

I'm the only one with the right to breach the fortress of his intimacy. He shows no revulsion when I help him dress or undress. He allows me to use the comb, the scissors, the razor blade. After many months of practice, he can now use the toothbrush with his left hand once I squeeze toothpaste onto it. He knows he has to recover some autonomy, as I'm not always around to help him out. It's time he started to grow up.

Billy is running around the Christmas tree, but he isn't touching the presents. He has a good personality, quite restrained. Sake would have messed up the gifts completely by this time. Billy is wise enough to mind his own business. Like Adam, he needs encouragement to perform new tricks.

We eat our breakfast at the living room table. Usually we sit at the kitchen counter, but today I feel like a little formality. I cut two slices of bread, spread one with pâté, the other with honey, and put them on Adam's plate, next to his cup of tea.

A few months ago, I reduced his coffee intake. Does he remember that he used to drink a whole pot of coffee? He has never complained about the tea he now drinks morning and evening.

I ask him, "Do you like tea, Adam?"

I have asked him this many times before.

"Yes," he says without looking at me.

"Do you know what I put in it today?"

"No."

"It's easy, though. Try again."

He takes a sip to please me, but he's uncomfortable. He knows this is a test.

Will he pass?

Not this time. It's so easy, though. It's mint. What could be easier than recognizing mint in a cup of tea?

"It's mint, Adam. From our garden."

He understands he flunked the test, and he's devastated. My voice leaves him feeling it was stupid of him not to guess the right answer. He searches for some excuse to look at the garden through the living room doors. Then he looks at me. Is he checking to see if I'm making fun of him? Should I say I picked the mint this morning, just to tease him?

I decide to come clean; I have a long day ahead of me.

"I kept it in the freezer, Adam."

Now he understands and is happy. He calmly takes a mouthful from his cup, then another and another. He's using a technique he learned at the Geriatric Centre, repeating again and again things he particularly wants to keep in mind. From now on, he absolutely wants to remember that I can trap him with tea made with mint picked in summer and kept in the freezer over the winter.

Billy settles at our feet hoping for some crumbs – another bad habit he learned from us. Ana told me never to feed him while we're eating, as he'll get bolder and bolder, standing up on his hind legs and staring at our plates.

I no longer care what Ana says. Billy is our guest, and I want him to feel welcome. I feed him whatever I'm eating – bread, pâté, cheese. Adam pats him.

"Who would have thought?" I ask myself: Adam patting a dog and still eating.

He was always revolted by filth, bad smells, and animals. He could walk a dog but would never touch it. When he got home with Sake or Billy, I always had to be the one who cleaned their paws. Today, he spoils Billy with bits of bread that he puts directly in his mouth, which means touching Billy's lips. Before his stroke, this would have been unthinkable, but now I let him do it. I've had enough of Adam's physical fastidiousness, which dates back to when he was diagnosed with hepatitis.

I stack the dishes, wash them, and set them on the rack to dry.

I'm going to finish up the shopping today. This year, I've had trouble deciding what to buy the kids. It's been as difficult as choosing Adam's gift. What's toughest of all, though, is advising the kids what to get him. They know they can no longer give him the same kinds of things they used to buy, but then what? Pencils? Drawing pads? A cartoon book?

Sara suggested a new video game. She said it would keep him busy when I'm out. I hesitated to tell her that, although her father may well have the intelligence of a ten-year-old boy, he doesn't have the same interests. If he has lost the abilities he once had, surely he must have retained some trace of the man he used to be? His brain is marked forever by so much of what he experienced in the past: I just can't believe the man he was is completely gone.

This is what I hope, anyway. I'm still waiting for the day when Adam wakes in the morning, making the gestures he used to make, saying the words he used to say. I want to forget the day I called Sara to let her know her father was lying in bed, empty-eyed. More than anything, I would like to erase the memory of the ride in the ambulance, the sound of the siren, and the hours spent waiting for the doctor to tell me the news. I want to forget how many days I kept the lunchbox I had prepared for him the night before he had his stroke.

I ask Adam if he wants to come shopping with me. I'm sure he'll say yes; he doesn't like being alone in the house.

I get him dressed and wait for the car to warm up. Billy starts rolling around on the rug. He thinks we're going out again. I watch him compassionately. Poor thing. Not wise enough in spite of his bushy white eyebrows.

At the mall, I leave Adam on a bench under a huge plastic palm tree; I have to go from shop to shop, and he would slow me down. I remind him of the small plastic card hanging around his neck. If he were ever to get lost, the card would tell whoever finds him about his condition and provide contact details for Sara and me.

From time to time, I stop to look at him from behind the racks of merchandise outside the stores. From a distance, he looks just as bored as the other men waiting for their wives to finish their shopping. I try to read the way he moves, the ways he looks. I still think he's making fun of me. I still hope he'll turn to me and say some silly thing, the way he always used to. I follow the direction of his eyes, to see if he's looking at the women parading past him with their gaudy shopping bags. And yes, he does look at them. Half-paralyzed though he is, he's still just like other men who check out young women's breasts and buttocks – never at their faces.

The shopping takes me two hours. When I'm done, I collapse on the bench next to Adam. He's happy to have me back. He doesn't need to tell me how worried he was. I can read the fear on his face.

Is he able to imagine the worst? That I leave and never return? Or, less dreadfully, that I leave and strangers ask questions in a language he no longer understands, search his pockets, find the plastic card with his information, and call me to rescue him. He has reason to be afraid.

I lead him to the café in the middle of the mall, a counter with a few tables and potted cypresses, and order a coffee and a slice of date cake for me, a cup of tea and chocolate cake for him. I could have chosen date cake for him too, that would be a lot healthier than the greasy chocolate cake he likes. But, what the hell, it's Christmas.

I show him what I've bought. A silk scarf for Ana and a pair of moccasins for her husband George. For Sara I decided on ruby earrings. She's a dentist, and earrings are the only jewelry she can wear, so she likes to have lots to choose from. I explain to Adam why this is the best present for her. He agrees. I bought leather gloves for Michael; Sara had told me he'd lost his old ones. I got cozy black and grey pyjamas for Adam. I urge him to touch the fabric and check its softness. He smiles at me happily.

Outside it feels colder, the sun glinting off the ice, the wind stronger than it was. Adam can't keep up with me as I walk over to the car on the far side of the parking lot, so I tell him to wait inside. He says he prefers to stay outdoors. I wonder if it's here that he fears being abandoned – fears I'll take the car and drive off, and he'll just wait and wait until he turns to ice.

At home, it's nice and warm. I turned up the heat up before we went out; I want to do some cooking and baking in comfort. The windows are still frosted over, though, except for the ones in our bedroom, which face southwest. This side of the house gets the sun once the trees lose their leaves in the fall.

I chop. I grind. I mince. I fry. I boil. Adam sits at the big table in the living room and draws.

The kitchen has always been my domain. Adam never much enjoyed everyday cooking, not for lack of interest but because he thinks preparing food is women's work. Back home in Romania, his mother, who's now seventy-seven, is still in charge of feeding the whole family. It was rare that Adam took over in the kitchen. He only did so when I was sick or, very rarely, when I was just fed up.

He used to have an uncanny knack of knowing when the sight of the sink, the tea-towels, the stove, the drawers, the kitchen utensils, the bags of vegetables, and the cans of beans and tomatoes would make me sick. When that happened, he knew he had to put on an apron and open up the old cookbook we brought over with us. The name on the cover is a woman's, but the book was written by a man. It was thought that no publisher would stand for a man writing a book of recipes.

I just use it to check the ingredients for some traditional dishes. When Adam did cook, he used to go through the old recipes calmly, following outdated instructions for beating eggs with a fork and kneading dough by hand, the book having been written before there were appliances for those kinds of things.

The meals he came up with were always good, though. He put a lot of effort into making them, and he never took his eyes off the pan — not even for a second. He hovered beside the stove until the meal was ready, tasting the food every few minutes to check if the seasoning was right. The length of time it took him to put together a stew was enough to guarantee he would not be cooking often. And after a day or two I always got over my neurosis and got back to work. The women in my family had never complained about spending too long in the kitchen, and I wasn't one to break with tradition.

When it came to the holidays, though, Adam had always been happy to get involved in the preparations. Christmas was a nostalgic part of our childhood and our shared past. He liked to breathe in the smell of fat sausages, boiled sauerkraut, cakes baking in the oven. There were too many vegetables for one person to chop anyway, so he used to cut up the onions, the carrots, and the cabbage, leaving me the task of rolling the cabbage rolls — *sarmale* — and kneading the dough. Now, with his right arm paralyzed, he can no longer handle food preparation.

Friends call to wish me Merry Christmas and ask for news about

Adam. These conversations annoy him, as they hold up my work. He doesn't raise his head from his drawings, but I can tell what he thinks from the ways he furrows his eyebrows. Adam is right; I have to keep working. I keep at it, with the phone wedged between my ear and my shoulder.

Sara calls to ask if I need help, but she knows I can handle it on my own. I've always managed the birthday parties and the big dinners.

In the afternoon, a sore back forces me to lie down on the couch. I don't know what causes the pain, but it dates back to my childhood. When I stand for too long in a certain position, a terrible ache seizes the left side of my back, near the bottom of my ribcage. The idea of seeing our family doctor about this terrifies me. So far, she has not even managed to figure out the cause of my stomach aches. The specialists have done no better, so I don't exactly relish the idea of starting again with a different complaint. I suffer from pains nobody can cure, and I just have to accept this. I prefer to keep them to myself.

One of my friends, who is a doctor, thinks my bones and muscles must have developed unevenly when I was growing up. When the bones grow first, everything's fine, but if the muscles develop faster and the skeleton is not strong enough to support them, the result can be a bad back and even nausea. I think this must be what happened, for my spine has been slightly bent since I was eleven. Nowadays, I get tired and have trouble walking.

It may be the weight I've gained. I've only put on seven pounds since I was in my thirties, but even that makes a difference. I'm not going to diet, though; I've always known my looks would change with age.

My godmother once told me we don't get fatter; we get bigger. I was young then, but she was a wise woman, and she wanted to prepare me for a terrible autumn ahead. She said, "Look at a young

10

tree and then at an old one — the trunks, the branches, the bark. You see the difference, don't you? No living creature can stand in the way of age. Trees don't know about diets; they wear their age beautifully. We should do the same."

Mentally, I've been ready to grow old ever since I was thirty, but not physically.

The sense of well-being that suddenly comes over me makes me forget my backache. The house is neat, the saucepans are ready on the counter, the cake is in the oven. I light three scented candles to cover up the kitchen smells. Boiled cabbage is always the worst; it even finds it way into the bedroom.

Billy is asleep on his pillow. I think he's eaten too much, and I'm a little worried. George warned me not to give him too much to eat, as he doesn't know when to stop.

We settle down in the living room to watch a movie. Adam is lying on his sofa and I on mine. I give him the sheepskin to lay over the cold leather of the couch. I use a wool blanket.

Billy leaves his pillow and comes over, looking for company. He stands close to my face until I look at him, then takes the small smile that spreads across my face as an invitation to jump up on the sofa and curl up behind me, his muzzle on my thigh.

Adam looks more handsome than he used to. These days, his hair is always perfectly cut because I take him to the hairdresser every month. The whiskers of his ears and nostrils are regularly clipped, as are his nails; he doesn't have to put up with my reproaching him about any of that any more. Even his beard is now properly trimmed, and his Adam's apple and the top of his cheeks scrubbed clean.

He's lost weight too, and looks healthier. He looks younger than I do. I don't know if he knows I dye his hair. He did ask me once what I was doing, and I told him I was treating him for hair loss. When he looked in the mirror afterwards, the first time, the result made him smile.

He really is handsome. His lips are as rosy and tender as those of a young man. He's lost the dark rings under his eyes and the nicotine spots on his teeth. Since Sara is our dentist, she does his cleaning twice a year and checks for cavities. Before, it was very difficult to get Adam to a dentist unless he had a toothache.

Our new hairdresser, a Hungarian woman, plays an important role in this metamorphosis. I've given her creative licence to try out fashionable cuts on Adam, and I never question what she does. Ilona is more than a hairdresser; she's become a friend.

I discovered her by chance one day when I went to have the battery in my watch changed at a jewelry store next to her salon. She was sitting in the back, filing her nails. I went in and explained Adam's condition, said I was looking for a very patient person to cut his hair. I also added that Adam hated to be touched, which was why he always used to delay getting a haircut. I wanted to prepare her for the way he might react.

Ilona cut me off before I was finished, saying that Adam could complain all he wanted and she wouldn't mind. She would gladly take him on and promised he would end up looking like a movie star.

One month, she let his bangs grow on the left, the next time on the right. Once, she even shaved his sideburns. This Nazi hairdo didn't suit him, though, because he has a flat head. Two days later, I went back to Ilona and asked her to change the look, and she did, for free.

Ilona was born in Hungary, and when she moved to Canada she married a man who said he was a Hungarian born in Transylvania. What's odd is that he speaks neither Romanian nor Hungarian. He had come to Canada when he was very young, apparently, and his parents had been so keen to assimilate that they refused to pass their heritage onto their children. Ilona didn't agree with this. She peppered her English liberally with Hungarian words no one else could understand. I didn't dare ask what language she and her husband used with one another. For some immigrants, language is as sensitive a subject as sex.

With Adam, she used even more Hungarian, for he didn't react in any way. *"Hercegem. Minden nö szìvét össze fogod törni."**

When we first went to her, Ilona would explain what she was planning for Adam's hair, and I would translate for him. After a bit, though, I insisted she communicate with him directly, with gestures. Or she could say nothing. I wanted to be left alone while she did her work, a few minutes to myself to sip her diluted coffee and flip through her well-thumbed magazines.

Ilona now talks directly to Adam and doesn't seem to care that he doesn't understand a word. She's just pleased to have such a nice, quiet customer. Adam is uncomfortable with her chattiness. A visit

---

*   *My prince. You will break every woman's heart.*

to Ilona terrifies him as much as an appointment with the doctor. I'm sure he would prefer another hairdresser, but I feel good here, and it's close to home.

On a Wednesday afternoon in late January, I had a phone call from Peter, and I didn't tell Adam. I was worried the news would bother him.

It's only this evening, in front of the TV, that I mention it. "Do you remember Peter?" I ask.

Adam takes a long time to search deep inside his puzzled memories, but comes out empty-handed. He needs more help.

"Peter and Lara were our neighbours. In Bucharest, we lived in the same building but on different floors. They have twin daughters. He used to teach at the university, and she had an accounting job with a foreign company. Lara's family was close to yours. Do you remember them?"

Adam badly wants to please me, so he pretends to remember them. This is the clearest indication that he doesn't. He wishes I would abandon this line of questioning, but I keep going.

"They left for the US two years before we came here. He got a grant to do his post-doctorate somewhere in the south. Lara and the girls followed him after a bit."

These details don't help. Adam accepts his defeat grudgingly. He decides to be fair and acknowledge the big gap in his memory. "Were we good friends?"

"Yep."

He tries even harder to focus. He's been practising a new way of fighting his weakness, taking different paths into the darkness of his brain. When he badly wants some result, he knows that asking the right questions could help.

"How come his name is Peter? Is that a Romanian name?"

"He's Russian," I answer. "Lara went to complete her Bachelor's degree in Moscow, and that's where she met Peter. This was during the Communist regime. They got married and moved to Bucharest. Peter always dreamt of going back to Moscow, but he didn't trust Putin. In the end, they moved to the States."

"Where are they now, then?" he asks, confused.

His question surprises me. Does he know the difference between the United States and Canada? Did he get that far with his geography lessons?

"They're in Montreal," I tell him. "He finished his post-doctorate south of the border and now has a teaching job at Concordia. They moved here a few years ago, bought a house on the South Shore. One of their daughters got married, and the other one is still living at home. Their girls are a bit older than Sara."

Adam is happy to track down this new lead, a good reason to continue the discussion in a manageable way. "Are they old?"

"No, not really. He'd be about fifty-three. And she's fifty, about the same age as you, if I remember correctly."

Adam stays quiet for a while. This makes me believe he is finally looking in the right place to trace them. His silence is a sign that he's sniffing around, like a dog following a thief. He's close to locating them in the ruined maze of his mind. The problem is, he can enter this labyrinth, but he can't find his way out again.

I let him rummage around in his memories for a while, but his silence eventually makes me think he may be moving away from the initial question. I bring him back to the starting point, "They want to come over one of these days."

This news makes Adam miserable. He knows that every new visit is about him. Everybody wants to see him. He thought he had dealt with them all, but no, there are new people who will not leave us alone, new faces that will stare at him. Tears well up in his eyes.

"Do they know?" he asks me in a desperate voice.

"Of course they know, Adam."

He waits for me to make a decision, as usual, but this time I stall, waiting for his reaction. I need this reaction. After five minutes though, I resign myself to the fact that there won't be one. Either he has completely forgotten that I'm waiting for an answer, or he imagines I've gone ahead and made a decision without him.

I decide to leave him alone watching the news. Yet a few minutes later, he switches to *Animal Planet*. I marked this channel with a red marker on the remote, so he can easily find the wildlife documentaries he likes so much. As long as he has the remote, he knows he can choose whatever he wants. Lately, nothing interests him as much as the silence of wild animals, even when the narrator is speaking a language he doesn't understand.

Oddly enough, he remembers Romanian and a bit of French, but no English. I put this down to the common origins of the Latin languages. Adam thinks it's very bad that he can't speak anything other than Romanian. He relaxes a bit when I remind him that he did a Master's degree in French and a PhD in English and that he was perfectly trilingual before his stroke. I have even complimented him and told him that his English was better than mine, for he used to work for a Swedish company. Since then, whenever he feels uncomfortable in front of our guests, he tells them, "I did a Master's degree in French and a PhD in English."

This is an attempt to wipe out the shame of forgetting.

A few days after this, I have to tell Adam that Peter absolutely insisted on visiting us. He wanted us to get together at their place on the South Shore, but I told him Adam has trouble with new places. I also lied and said we don't visit anyone now, except our daughter.

I don't know why I keep justifying this decision to Adam. This is not the first time he's had to agree to see strangers who were once friends. I could reassure him the way I usually do, tell him everybody is already aware of his condition, nobody will ask a lot of questions.

Sometimes this works, but not always. There are people who make him very uncomfortable, even if they ignore him. Others he finds more bearable, even likeable. I can tell from the way he makes eye contact with them. He even talks about his diplomas and shows them his dead arm. What humiliates him is the fact that he doesn't speak either French or English, not that anyone expects him to.

What Adam does not know is that the prospect of having Peter and Lara over for dinner makes me even more anxious than him.

I can't even imagine how they'll look after all these years. Or how shocked they'll be to see how we've changed.

I decide not to agonize too much over the preparations. I don't want to make Adam even more worried by paying too much attention to their visit. I vacuum, dust, wash the ceramic floors in the hall, and leave the windows open for half an hour to let fresh air in, despite the terrible cold.

17

I do battle with the smells of illness and ageing. I change the sheets and Adam's pyjamas twice a week. I bought him both coloured and white pairs so I could wash them every time I put on a load of laundry. Yet the smells are impregnated in the walls, in the rug, in the curtains, and in our closet.

Adam knows it's his fault the windows are open in the dead of winter.

We do our grocery shopping at the usual places: Adonis, Transylvania, IGA. He knows the routine by heart. I make a point of putting the usual items in the shopping cart so there's no reason for Adam to think there's anything special about this visit.

For this unwanted get-together, I decide to go with my usual guest meal: a veal soup to start with and a main course of pork with peas and dill. As I'm cooking, though, I realize the piece of meat is too big and too lean, and it will get tough before it's cooked through. I try to do something about this by cutting small holes in the pork and filling them with slivers of bacon and garlic. For dessert, I make a flan. This is a failure, too. The missing ingredient is the soul, as my mother would have said.

I make sure to finish the preparations before the guests arrive, and then I settle in on the couch, next to Adam, and pretend to watch TV. This is enough for him to forget we're expecting company.

When the bell rings, he looks at me anxiously. I reassure him. "Here they are. Just in time." I remind Adam who our guests are. He stands up, the remote still in his hand.

As I open the door, I understand what Adam goes through each time he finds himself in front of people he doesn't recognize any more. I'm even more shocked than he is, and I probably don't hide it very well.

Lara leads the way, up to her nose in an expensive fur coat. Peter's face is hidden behind a huge bouquet of roses.

Adam looks more confident than I do. He's unexpectedly calm. Does he understand that this couple has nothing in common with us any more?

Lara is very slim, and her dress fits tightly around her waist. Despite her youthful figure (no doubt she's on a strict diet), her waxy face gives her age away, as does the fan of wrinkles around her mouth, which get deeper when she moves her lips. Her hair is arranged in an elegant bun on top of her head.

Peter can only be described as obese. His handsome Russian face has morphed into a shiny, double-chinned mask, and there are dark circles around his once soulful eyes. His hair is still long, but this makes its sparseness the more noticeable.

They ask for white wine, and I have a gin and tonic with lots of ice and lemon. No other drink puts me at ease in social situations while keeping me alert enough to manage the whole evening. This time though, its effect seems to be delayed. We're perching on the sofas, and our guests are staring at the walls, the rug, the paintings – anything to avoid looking at Adam.

"Wow. You decorated the house in the Romanian style," Lara says with false admiration.

Judging by her lavish personal style, I know our modest furnishings can't possibly impress her.

"What's wrong with that?" asks Peter in a thin voice.

"I didn't say it was wrong." Lara laughs nervously.

I look around the room, trying to see what they see. There's a Romanian tapestry in the hall that Adam's mother gave us years ago, and painted plates from Horezu. In the corners of the living room, we have big blue and white pottery from the Transylvanian village of Konrod. It's cluttered, I know. A guest once asked me if it was difficult keeping so much pottery from breaking, given Adam's condition. I answered that Adam knows not to play football indoors.

Lara wants to know how I was able to get all this stuff over here.

"Bit by bit," I say.

"But carrying so many things on your own?"

"Adam has not been ill forever, as you know."

Peter jumps in to rescue Lara, though her remarks have clearly made him uncomfortable.

"Do you go back much?" he inquires politely.

"Not any more."

Lara chimes in to tell me they haven't been back at all, and they have no intention of doing so. They prefer to invite their families to visit them — one year the Romanians, the next the Russians.

I can tell Peter is dying to address Adam in some way, but he doesn't know how. The only progress he's made is that he's trying to make eye contact.

It's as though Adam has taken Peter's gaze as some kind of judgment. "I no longer understand French or English," he says.

Lara bursts out laughing. She then apologizes, which is worse. Peter is mortified, but Adam's comment unnerved him, too. I think he wonders if Adam is making fun of them.

I try to remedy the situation. "That's not true Adam, you do understand a little French, and you have made great progress with your English."

He makes a "so-so" motion with his hand, but I know my interjection makes him proud. To make him feel even better, I tell Peter, "Adam did a Master's degree in French and a PhD in English."

I ask everyone to come over to the table. The soup is mild and the flavour of lovage quite pronounced. Even the roast is better than I expected. What they seem to appreciate most is the dill with peas, as though they had never come across this combination before, even though it's common back home.

Lara eats voraciously, as though trying to convince me she

comes by her slim figure naturally. This idea occurs to me when she says that everyone at work envies her body. Peter takes a long break after every bite. For God knows what reason, the food seems too big a snake for him to swallow. He apologizes for his lack of appetite, saying he just ate with his daughter and her new boyfriend. Lara eats even more aggressively, which makes me believe this is a lie.

"You could drink a bit," she says to Peter. "I'll drive us home."

Is this an allusion to Peter drinking too much? That would explain his ruined body.

Peter grabs his glass of wine to cover his embarrassment.

The conversation falters, which puts Adam on his guard: he knows something is wrong with these people. Usually, our guests are much more talkative. After the soup course and a few more glasses of wine, everyone forgets about Adam in his corner of the table, everyone but me of course. He can comfortably eat and listen to the sound of their voices, because he doesn't register much of what people are saying. I think he feels like some kind of blob.

When we're at dessert, Lara accepts a liqueur, which prompts Peter to warn her that she's had enough to drink.

She responds violently. "I do not need to be told what to do. And for God's sake, not about drinking."

So I was right. Peter does drink too much.

I think even Adam has figured out this evening's mystery: this is not a happy couple. He doesn't understand what's lurking behind each word, but the tone of their voices leaves him in no doubt. Lately, he has developed a flawless ear for any hint of adversity. This is his only defensive weapon.

He lowers his head, which is a sign of great fear. I don't want the others to notice his sudden withdrawal, so I try to come up with a new topic of conversation. Yet, my goodness, how difficult it is to talk to these people.

I'm greatly relieved when Lara stands up and announces they're going to be on their way. At the door, we all pretend to be cold so that our farewells will be brief.

When I get back to the living room, Adam starts crying. He puts his good arm around my shoulders and leans his head against mine. I feel like crying, too, but I try to stay strong. "They're gone," I say. "Don't worry about it. They'll never be back, I promise."

While I get ready for bed in the bathroom, Adam gets undressed by himself. He even folds his clothes and puts them on the chair next to his nightstand. When I come into the bedroom, he's struggling with the last button of his pyjama top.

"I got your toothbrush ready," I tell him, rubbing his good arm.

He looks at me happily and heads for the bathroom.

Marta invites us to her fiftieth birthday party, and I know we have to go. When friends throw a party in their home, we usually go for two or three hours, max. This time, though, Marta has rented a Greek restaurant for the evening, which means there'll be lots of people, and we might be stuck there for an indeterminate amount of time.

I tell Adam the news, and he does not react. He knows Marta, for she drops by quite often, but he doesn't remember the details of their long friendship: that they grew up in the same neighbourhood and went to the same university, that their parents are still on good terms. Marta is the most attentive of our friends. She calls every weekend to ask for updates on Adam's condition and often invites us to join them for outdoor activities and barbecues. Every time she organizes a family supper she invites us, even when her daughter's in-laws, who only speak English, will be there.

Marta is a social butterfly, the key link between different groups and subgroups of our community. In her house, she gathers young and old, people of all professions and all regions of Romania. She favours people from the south, invites fewer Moldavians (they're not funny enough) and even fewer Transylvanians (they're too proud). We've nicknamed her Big Brother, and tease her about her nosiness. Despite her inquisitiveness, she chooses her words very carefully when she does ask questions, doing her best to avoid sensitive issues. Curious as she is, it may be that Marta is actually less informed than the rest of us. I have a suspicion that she doesn't really want to know too much. She's so generous that she'd feel obliged to rescue everyone, if she knew the details, and that would be too much, even for her.

Marta's tolerance does have its limits. She would see not going to her birthday celebration as a terrible offence, even with Adam as an excuse.

I drive to work today because I want to go to the mall on my way home and get a present for Marta. I'm not going to get her clothes or perfume, which are the hardest things to buy for someone else and, in our circle, the items most likely to be re-gifted. What we don't like, we recycle. We wait patiently for the birthday of someone who is not a close friend to get rid of the unwanted gift. We even recycle the wrappings, which we fold carefully and put away neatly so they won't get crumpled. We are masters in the art of gift recycling.

This year, I decide on a broach in the shape of a dragonfly with two pairs of wings, one in silver, the other in amber. Marta always compliments me on my jewelry, so I hope she won't want to give this away to someone else.

Getting ourselves dressed on Saturday evening requires some thought, especially for Adam. Before, he would never go out without a suit on, so I had to adapt my style to his own. The sober colours of his suits and ties forced me to wear clothes I didn't like.

I've had to change his wardrobe since his stroke, and I've bought him clothes I like – black jeans, turtlenecks, velvet jackets, and wool coats. In winter, he even wears scarves that match the colour and fabric of his coat, gloves and hat. So far, I haven't had the heart to throw away his old suits, jackets, shirts and ties, but I have relegated them to the back of the closet, packed away in plastic boxes.

I set out brown cords for him, a beige shirt and a Shetland wool sweater. The clothes fit him so well that I'm envious.

For myself, I decide on a green jersey dress and my black velvet coat. This goes perfectly with my Damaskin broach and the Mallorca pearls I bought during our trip to Spain a few years back. I pull on thick stockings and my high-heeled suede boots, which will give me a good excuse not to dance.

I have to warm the car up for more than ten minutes to defrost the sheet of ice on the windows. Adam waits on the sofa while I watch through the window for the moment when the windshield clears.

Adam is always anxious before this kind of gathering. To reassure him, I explain who we're going to see, how long we're going to spend there, and what will be expected of him. He understands that his condition has turned him into a sort of attraction, and this makes him uncomfortable. He would happily avoid social occasions.

This reluctance to socialize, however, isn't just the result of his new condition. He never tired of staying home, always suffering from some degree of agoraphobia. We were afraid of what our friends would think if we never went on vacation, so we did sometimes go away. The holiday Adam always liked best, though, was to stay home and sleep in every day. What could be better than not having to get dressed in the morning and fight your way through traffic to get to work?

A vacation was a nightmare for him, everything about it – choosing the place, making the bookings, dealing with luggage, the airport, the flights, the hotel, jetlag, doing as much as possible for the price we paid. The few times we stayed home, just driving out to the country – to the Gaspé or Charlevoix – were always the most enjoyable vacations. The most exhausting trips were to Europe, and the dullest were at those indistinguishable sunshine destinations.

No one judges us any more. Adam always had poor social skills. It was rare for him to form a connection with anyone.

He always used to be bored at parties. Two hours after we got there, he would start gravitating towards the door. I was a little uncomfortable in social situations, too, but unlike Adam, I loved listening to the talk around me. When I went to dance, I had to do it in a group, because Adam hated dancing. He was naturally shy and avoided any kind of public exhibition. The only times we ever danced together were in our youth, when he was wooing me. I'm the only person who knew he was not a bad dancer.

In Marta's group, there was just one person who was more introverted than Adam, an eternal PhD student in sociology. He didn't even make the effort to stay with the others, but settled on his own in a corner or watched TV in the living room. I think everyone wondered why he bothered to come to these parties. Adam and I wanted to avoid this kind of judgment.

When we arrive at the restaurant, the entrance hall is already full of people. I would have preferred to arrive earlier, to avoid having everyone's gaze fixed on Adam, but I missed the exit on the highway. With all the snow and cold, I should have accepted a friend's offer of a ride, but this would have meant staying on until they were ready to leave. I don't want to stay more than three hours, to the end of the main course.

Daniel wants to help Adam with his coat, but I signal that Adam can handle this by himself. I don't intervene until he has to take off his boots. His party shoes, perfectly waxed, are under the big galoshes he's now finally willing to wear.

How many times we used to fight over those bloody galoshes. He never wanted to wear them, thinking they made him look like a frogman. Avoiding ridicule was more important to him than damaging his leather shoes, and I was the one, anyway, who had to polish and wax them. Now, he doesn't care.

We've been placed at Dora and Virgil's table along with two couples we don't see very often. The music is way too loud for conversation.

26

We can exchange only a few words during short breaks when the DJ shows a slideshow of photos of Marta at every age. Everybody exclaims at these, mostly about how thin we all used to be. Adam is now in better shape than any of the others, and they envy him that, in spite of everything.

After the aperitifs and the appetizers, I tell Adam I'm going to dance. He nods his head. In the middle of the hall, people are dancing energetically, especially the women, whose tight black dresses still fit them perfectly since they haven't eaten yet. I'm surprised at all this activity, for I know they all saw one another recently enough. These are people who have been spending New Year's Eve in one another's company for years now.

Half an hour later, I look over to our table and see Adam sitting alone, watching the dancers as if he fears being caught in the act. When he's on his own, everybody avoids him. Yet going back to him right now would turn us into a really pathetic couple. I stay on the dance floor for one more song, until I can take advantage of a blues track to sit with Adam again.

Our table is one of the first to be served. Adam can't manage a knife, so I cut the meat on his plate. After months of physiotherapy, he can still only hold the fork in his left hand. Our neighbours watch discreetly to see if Adam drools. I could reassure them that he does not. Adam eats as daintily as he always did. I always envied his style and the patience with which he chews his food. The stroke has not deformed him; on the contrary, it has actually fixed a slight asymmetry in his face. This evening, his hair has been well coiffed by Ilona, who promised he would break the ladies' hearts.

Our friends come over to greet us, exchange a few words, and ask Adam a few questions. He's coy in front of so many faces and names he doesn't remember, and this makes him look wise. People are not fully aware of the gravity of his condition and imagine he can still engage in a conversation on industry, politics, and the price of gasoline. His silence fools them; they interpret it as discretion or thoughtfulness rather than incomprehension.

Men soon make their farewells with an affable slap on his back or, even worse, on his paralyzed arm. Women are more persistent. They don't give up that easily, not before hearing Adam articulate a few words, at least. I try to save him by dominating the discussion. Adam has the habit of nodding at each of my words, which might suggest to the others that he's listening and participating.

I know this is not really so, for he has more difficulty with my explanations than with their questions. The only time he can follow is when I explain the stroke. He has heard this account so many times that he knows all the details. He listens to them with pleasure.

Three hours later, we've had enough, Adam and I. I have some difficulty saying goodbye to so many people, and Marta takes charge of doing it for me. She even remarks that we stayed longer than usual. She promises to drop by tomorrow and bring us some cake, if there's any left.

Back at home, as we're getting undressed, Adam asks, "Did I used to dance?"

"Yes," I reply, unfastening his belt. "You were the best dancer. We even danced in the middle of the circle. We danced in front of everybody from the beginning of the evening right to the end."

"Are you sure I was that good?"

"I'm positive. You were the best."

Would he like to dance now? Maybe I should give it a try at the next party. We don't have to move quickly across the dance floor. Despite his paralyzed foot, we could do some bluesy moves. I could even request some songs we used to love.

Otherwise, I will never have the chance to dance to the blues again, because no one dares to ask me. That would be seen as either pity or flirting. Nobody is so unloved in a circle of married couples as a single woman, and I look available. I have no trouble understanding the look I now see on the faces of old friends, their insinuations, and the exaggerated attention I get from people I only ever exchanged a few words with before.

These are all people we met after we got here. We met them through Marta, who already had a wide circle of friends. She and Daniel came here five years before us, time enough to smooth out a few rough edges. They introduced us to everybody who could share their experiences with us, or help us if need be. Some of them helped us buy our first car, and some gave us sticks of furniture they no longer wanted – towels, pots, glasses, everything we needed for the months after our arrival.

Marta's circle has remained close, but we have also formed our own groups of friends among our work colleagues and people we met at other parties. We frequent Marta's circle whenever we're invited. At the start, there were new faces every season. Then some of them began to argue or they decided they couldn't stand one another any more. Lately, however, the rhythm has changed, and they've become a kind of extended family. Without parents, brothers or sisters, they all spend Christmas, New Year's, and Easter together and go to all the same birthday parties, weddings, and christenings.

In the last few years, illnesses have slowly started to infiltrate the group, but we haven't experienced a funeral. No one our age has yet died, though Marta's best friend's son was killed in a car accident. A few months later, the mother stopped coming to our get-togethers, and Marta never spoke about it.

A bunch of them also go on vacation together, but we've managed to avoid that, coming up with all kinds of excuses. We've never been sociable enough to consider spending a whole week in the same company. Neither Adam nor I can hold a conversation for very long, and prolonged contact with the same people makes us both uncomfortable. It used to embarrass us that we were so boring.

The real solidarity has always been between the two of us. Adam and I felt good together. It was as though the presence of other people disturbed our subtle chemistry. We were not a perfect couple, but Adam could never stay away from home for long. He was made for family. On business trips, he used to call home twice a day, morning and evening, depending on his schedule and the time difference. He needed to feel the homey atmosphere that he missed. Foreign places disgusted him. He was chronically constipated because of hotel bathrooms. He was horrified by the sink, the bathtub, the towels, the sheets. He cleaned everything he could clean before using it. He was afraid of new surroundings.

Adam's body has now become a perfect engine, functioning according to a very precise schedule. Nothing can disturb his daily routine. Except for the days when I give him some bad news about an upcoming party or an unexpected visitor, he always looks happy.

I have an appointment at noon today with the principal, Madame Lavoie, and the mother of one of my eighth grade students, David Chukhaib. My argument with him took place in the library over the subject of his oral presentation. I proposed that he research a local writer, comedian, artist, or singer, but he was keen to speak about a French rapper who swore all the time. I didn't want to take the issue to the principal, but the boy became more and more disobedient and rude, so I had no choice but to call his mother. She doesn't speak either French or English very well and has a hard time dealing with my calls.

At home, however, David gave his mother a very different version of our conflict, and she asked to see the principal and me. So this morning I found a note in my pigeonhole about the noon meeting. I'm sure David will try to save himself by blaming me. Nothing new there.

In her office, Madame Lavoie gives me an opportunity to explain what happened. I tell her David refused to work on the topic I had proposed. Not only that, but he was caught looking at naked girls on the Internet. When I warned him that I would put him out in the corridor or even send him to the help room under the watchful eye of Mademoiselle Gingras, he got angry and refused to leave the computer. He didn't fancy spending an hour in the basement writing a hundred lines on good behaviour for Mademoiselle Gingras. When he got home, he accused me of psychological harassment.

The principal has no intention of ignoring the incident. She submits David to a close interrogation. She knows exactly how to get him to lose his temper. What she wants is to show David's mother his true nature. She starts by going over David's recent missteps, even getting him to admit to fighting with Muslim students over their religion. This is too much for David's mother, and she begs the principal to stop. A parent is often a great apologist for her children until they're charged with discrimination. In a nearly incomprehensible mix of French and English, David's mother shouts that her son is not stupid and that he speaks four languages. But Madame Lavoie tells her that David may have a conduct disorder; the school will soon have to set up an intervention plan and hire a specialist to accompany David to his classes. His last report card and this latest crisis are proof that he cannot be left on his own any more.

David starts stammering, which happens when he's nervous. His patience has reached its end. Mine has too, and the only way for me to wrap this up is to get David to promise he will change the French rapper for a Quebec one, and that he will come and see me over the lunch break in order to catch up with the others. He accepts these conditions because he has no intention of keeping his promises.

After school, I have to stay for the launch of Catherine's book. She's a colleague from the French department who has written a novel called *Twenty Days*. The launch, organized by our social committee, is from five o'clock to seven o'clock in the school basement. Half of the small space is taken up by a tomato garden, and the warmth from the grow lights and the moisture from the soil make the room feel like a greenhouse. The tables have all been covered in blue velvet for the occasion, and there are bowls with chips and glasses of sangria. I prefer to get myself a beer from the cash bar. I haven't been drinking beer lately, but this one hits the spot. It's been a long time since I had a glass without having to get one for Adam.

Oliver, the art teacher, sits down beside me. As usual, he has trouble because of his stiff leg, and his cane is an inconvenience when he wants to sit down. He has bought himself a beer, too, and he raises his glass, saying, "Cheers." I ask him if the students from my tutorial groups are still giving him trouble, and he smiles, saying this isn't the time to talk about it.

I'm so happy Annie-Claude comes over to sit with us. I like her, and I feel lucky this year to be the French tutor for some of her students. This is not the case with Robert's students, who have the same attitude as their teacher: distant, cold and disdainful. Annie-Claude's students are warm and affectionate.

I particularly like Sako, an Armenian from Lebanon, and Lissandra, a Colombian. I'm comfortable enough with them that they'll often stay to chat after class. They know my husband is unwell, and they always ask about him. Sometimes I sit in class with them during Annie-Claude's teaching hour to watch their progress and help them if they can't keep up. Annie-Claude is happy to have me in her classroom and wants to keep me as long as possible.

I don't think she can cope with such noisy classes. Today, she asked me to stay with her and give her a hand with the whole group on the introduction to a descriptive text on the 9/11 attacks. Sako showed me his draft, which went like this: "Across the world, there have been many tragic events, but those of 9/11 were unthinkable." I suggested he use the expression, "beggared description," and Sako was thrilled. He does not know many expressions in French: he arrived only recently and speaks only a little of this new language.

Annie-Claude is having a bad day. She did not sleep well last night, I can tell from the black circles under her eyes. I suspect it's the beginning of a breakdown. She lives alone with her fifteen-year-old son, and she gets depressed when it's time to fix something around the house. The current problem is a blocked chimney, and she keeps us posted on developments. Oliver teases her about the chimney. Robert, who is in charge of staging the evening, takes pictures of the three of us.

Catherine's book is about a young woman disguised as an old grandmother who works in a *crêperie*. A thick dress and some padding hide her fine skin, her long hair, her breasts and hips. No one could imagine what a beauty she really is, least of all the young man who sells cell phones on the other side of the lane. She's secretly in love with him, but the shop he works at is closing down in three weeks. This is all the time she has to win his heart.

It's late, but I don't go straight home. I have a terrible headache, and I want to take a walk in spite of the ice on the sidewalk. In the past few days, it snowed, then it rained, and now it's frozen over. I stop at the small park behind the school and sit on a bench. I get up to go when I start feeling cold.

It's dark when I get in. Adam has switched on the lamp in the living room and is waiting for me by the window. He can tell the time, but only sort of, so he draws big round clocks on a sheet of paper to mark the times of my departure and my arrival. I told him this won't really help him, as I often have to stay after school to finish my planning, meet the principal, or call parents. I always find him at the living room window, waving with his good hand as soon as I turn into the driveway.

Before I go indoors, I try to shovel away of the day's snow from the driveway, which has become a skating rink. I have to pay for my recent laziness. I should have swept away the puddles of water that have now frozen. The only good thing is that no one uses our driveway except me, and I know its worst spots well.

Adam welcomes me with the news that the telephone has rung five times; he has even noted this in his notebook. I pay no attention to his worry or to the blinking light that tells me there are messages. I sometimes wonder if anyone other than telemarketers care about us.

"Let me get changed, Adam, please. They can wait a while, unless you're waiting for a few calls."

He doesn't know how to react to this. I wish he would laugh, but he just looks at me in distress, and that fills me with horror. It's a long time since I've felt so down.

It's only after supper that I listen to the messages. There's one from Sara and one from Marta, and I can see Peter's family name on the display. I'm surprised I still remember it. He called twice, but left no message. I wonder if perhaps it's his name that made Adam anxious. Did Adam see his name? Did he recognize it?

I watch how seriously he's concentrating on his drawing, paying attention to each line of a winter landscape with children playing around a perfectly circular snowman.

Who gave him this book? My God, he isn't a child. The professionals at the Geriatric Centre say that adults underestimate the beneficial role played by colouring and drawing. Incredible as it may seem, small children can project themselves into the picture and breathe life into printed images. We should really be jealous of how they live inside their heads.

Is Adam a child who learns new things? Or is he an adult who has forgotten? To them it may be the same thing, but I think there's a big difference.

The telephone rings, startling me. I must have turned the volume up by mistake.

It's a Concordia University number.

Peter. He's calling me from his office. So he hasn't gotten home yet. Did he stay at work just to call me?

First, he asks me if I can talk. I say no, not really, but he continues anyway. I'm sure he understands Adam's limitations. Either it makes no difference to Peter if Adam's around, or he doesn't care how Adam will react.

Peter wants to set up a time for us to meet downtown and have a coffee. He wants to talk to me.

I tell him I have to get home after school to take care of Adam. He insists, but I stay firm. He says he can help me if I need any support. He adds that he imagines how difficult it must be for a woman to replace a man in the house.

"Difficult in what sense?" I ask in a bad temper. I explain as calmly as I can that if I have any problems, I call the plumber, the gardener, the snow cleaner, the electrician. I have a good salary and I can pay for any service I need to run my house. I add that Adam was never handy or fond of manual labour. He hated it when he really had no alternative but to take care of something. He fixed the faucets when the water was dripping because of the broken seals, and he ploughed the snow in the driveway when Canada Post threatened to sue us for putting its employees' lives in danger.

Peter is so insistent that I have to cut him off brusquely. "Listen, Peter, it isn't a man that's difficult to replace in a house. It's a husband."

That's the end of the conversation.

Adam used not to listen when I was on the phone, but he has been paying attention to this call. He heard the alarm in my voice. He set down his crayon and watched me the whole time.

"That was Peter," I say, taking a deep breath. "He insists on seeing me."

Adam does not dare ask why.

"He thinks I need his help."

Adam desperately wants to know what to say. I would like to end the conversation, but Adam hasn't yet picked up his crayon again.

What is he waiting for? There's nothing more to add.

Our weekend routine is the same as usual. I prepare the coffee, do my exercises, and then come back to the bedroom with a big mug. I turn on the lamp on my bedside table and read for an hour or two. The only magazine I still subscribe to is *Maclean's*, which I keep for Sundays. Even Adam used to leaf through it from time to time, without exactly loving it. He said he did not fit the profile of a *Maclean's* reader, but I've gotten used to its style, its articles, and its journalists.

Adam used to say that I read it because of my obsession with work well done, or perhaps with making the most of what I've paid for. He may be right. I can't bear to throw away a magazine I haven't read from cover to cover, including the ads.

One day, I even sent the magazine a letter criticizing a campaign launched by a fast food chain. In order to stimulate the sale of its products, the chain was advertising its support for research to fight stomach cancer, diabetes, and heart attacks. Isn't that the worst kind of hypocrisy, to sell poison and then pretend to look for the antidote?

Maclean's did not publish my letter, but they answered me privately, saying that the ads did not contravene any accepted ethical norms. I answered that if the ads did not contravene ethical norms, they certainly contravened good sense, but there was no reply.

As usual, I summarize some of the more intriguing news for Adam. Before his stroke, he was unwilling to listen. He was always exhausted after a week of hard work and just wanted to recuperate over the weekend. So I told him about the *Maclean's* article that argued an adult should sleep no more than seven hours a night.

These days, there's no need for me to lecture him. He's paid his sleep debts and rarely sleeps more than seven hours.

We've managed to cut out a whole bunch of other habits that used to cause us to fight. The most irritating was his habit of falling asleep in front of the TV. He was sometimes in the living room till midnight, when he would awaken with his kidneys frozen to the cold leather of the sofa. Too tired to brush his teeth and change into his pyjamas, he just came to bed in his T-shirt and shorts. After twenty years of marriage, I was still after him about his physical laziness and poor hygiene. Eventually I pretty much gave up, resigned in the face of all the evidence that a woman can never change her husband. Let him do as he pleased. A couple ends up getting its own particular habits, either through tolerance or through indifference.

Adam gets out of bed, brushes his teeth, and then lies down again next to me with his own book. He has learned the letters and is working on syllables. The fact that he has to learn two languages all over again complicates matters, the doctors all agree on that. They and I have decided, though, that he has to recreate the life he led before the stroke and try to relearn as much as possible. To keep track, I draw up school reports, three per year, which I complete after mid-term evaluations and final exams. He'll be on spring break at the same time as my students.

This morning, I tell him about an article on wearing the veil in Canada. He listens closely. Does he still think the veil should be banned in a secular society? That's what he used to think, before his stroke.

Today, I'm too drained to get into this.

We used to have hot-button issues that invariably ended in an argument. One was his admiration for Fidel Castro, who defied an empire as a young man, toppled an oppressive system, and reversed a colonial past. I pointed to Cuba's catastrophic history – living off the largesse of the Soviet Union, then abandoned after the fall of Communism – and its bleak future. How could heroism result in such a disaster? The Communist regimes excluded free will. That was the worst thing. People can't live without choice. Of course they're disappointed when a system that promised miracles proves to be a failure: that's been the case since the dawn of time. We're still living with the side effects, which include the demolition of self-esteem.

"The first communists, after all, were Athenian women," I used to say whenever Adam accused me of being an opportunist, by which he meant capitalist-lover.

I'm alone on the barricades now. Fidel Castro has turned into a senile old man in a blue tracksuit, and he haunts us no more. So I show Adam every article I see on the Cuban crisis and the problems all those old regimes now face. He listens in silence.

And since he's given up arguing, I start to give him a reason for doing so. In defending Cuba, he wanted to justify the twenty years we lived under Communism. Even if we deny Castro's achievements, we can't purge ourselves of our own Communist youth.

Adam dozes off, his children's book on his chest.

I watch the contortions of the wind-blown branches outside the window. It's stormy, the temperature just below zero. At the beginning of February the weather suddenly turned warm, and I've been able to walk to school, a ten-minute walk. The mountains of snow on the sidewalks are melting; the streets are being washed by rain. There was another shower this morning.

Heading back to the kitchen, I see our driveway is almost completely free of ice. And I thought I'd be dealing with a skating rink until spring. I don't use salt, which damages the roots of perennials along the edge of driveway and eats paving stones like a cancer.

Sara calls to ask if we want to go up north. I tell her I'm busy. Marta is organizing a party at her place just before Valentine's Day. She calls it a potluck community party, to disguise the fact we'll also be celebrating the pagan feast. She sent us all an email asking us each to make one dish. She'll take care of dessert, and wine will be $10 per person. According to her last message, though, it turns out that one of her friends has offered to contribute homemade wine. Everyone has to wear red.

On Friday morning, when I got Marta's message, I was in the staff room with a pile of exams. End of term is close, and I have a lot of marking to do, as well as reports to prepare for meetings with the parents. I answered, explaining it was impossible for me to get organized in time. She fired back, saying I didn't need to prepare anything. There'd be plenty of food.

I had my own reasons for declining the invitation. Preparing a dish for twenty or more is not such a big deal. What I don't like is the change to my routine.

On Saturdays, I usually spend the day cleaning and doing laundry. Sunday I shop and run errands. Adam likes to come along, this being the only time he leaves the house, except for outings he hates, like seeing the doctor, going to his old-and-forgotten-skills lessons, and visiting people he doesn't remember. He knows, too, that I never get back when I say I will, and he worries when I'm late. Our Sunday errands require nothing of him except to keep me company. No way he would miss out on them.

Marta's invitation wrecks my weekend.

We get out of bed at 8.30 a.m., dress for our outing, and have breakfast. I then warm up the car, in spite of the mild weather. This is what Stavros tells me to do; he's the mechanic who says I should never drive with a cold engine.

I follow professional advice religiously and would never disregard what a mechanic tells me. Stavros has had a lot of advice for me since Adam's stroke. He considers me pretty clueless when it comes to the car, but I can sometimes surprise him. Adam used to be terrific at deciphering car noises, every suspicious knock and clunk, and I learned how to recognize the difference between the sound of worn-out shock absorbers and the sound of snow tires against the chassis, which happens because they're bigger than regular tires. He also got me a shiny new tool case, which includes electrical chargers. I personally haven't needed them yet, but they've saved a few other people a bundle.

Stavros imagines that I owe all my mechanical knowledge to him. I do pretend that I understand what he mumbles in a mix of Greek and English. His garage has been one of the most dependable things in my life, but I fear now for Stavros's health, for the doctors have found a lump in his neck.

I take advantage of this early outing to stop at the Arab jewelry shop opposite Adonis on Curé Labelle. The receptionist called to let me know that my items were ready and the cost was $100, reasonable enough for three silver chains, a ring, a bracelet, and two new pairs of earrings – one with jade teardrops, the other with the transparent pink stone the Chinese call *shui jin*. These last are Sara's Valentine's Day presents.

The receptionist welcomes me warmly, turning away from the radio playing a song in Arabic. She seems to be overwhelmed. She hums along as she rummages through a box full of small, labeled plastic bags. I'm the only customer in the shop, which is full of perfume bottles and gold jewelry. There are swarms of people here during the holidays buying up cheap stuff. I don't trust her perfumes or her jewelry, either. I make a show of looking around, but this does not spark any interest. I probably don't look like the kind of person who wears big gold chains.

41

We cross the street to Adonis, which is jammed with people. At almost every counter, I hear people talking Romanian. I recognize one of my eighth grade students, Elena, with her mother. I avoid them, being in no mood for small talk.

Adam and I follow our usual route through the store. First stop is the meat counter, where I get some liver. The clerk behind the counter has figured out that something is wrong with my husband. He has seen him following me in his clumsy way, and he knows by now that his smile is not a happy one. He is Moroccan and lately he started flirting with me, killing me with his "Madame" this and "Madame" that. The other clerks see what he's doing and tease him. I don't mind his advances, if it means there'll be fewer gizzards mixed in with the liver.

Behind me, Adam pushes the shopping cart with his belly and his left arm. We move on for the cheese, sausages, olives, and finally coffee and peanuts. In the vegetable section, I pick up parsley and eggplant. The quality is good and the price is right, just $0.99 per lb. The fruit section is next. My God – apricots and cherries in wintertime. I stick to oranges, apples and pears.

At home, I unpack the car myself; it's too tricky to pick out the few items Adam could manage. We have bad memories of the day he fell on the ice with two jars of the vegetable spread *zacuska* and another jar of olives. He does rush to hold the door for me.

By three o'clock, I'm ready to start cooking. I'm making liver with tomato sauce and potatoes cooked the Transylvanian way – boiled in their skins, sliced into rounds, and fried with paprika.

At five, Marta calls to make sure I'm coming and to insist I not bring anything. I tell her I've already made it. She wants to send Daniel to help me out. I tell her there's no need, unless they want to give me a hand when I arrive at her house. I'm bringing the cast iron pot, which is heavy. She reminds me to wear something red.

Damn! I never wear red. If it hadn't been for this phone call, I could have pretended to have forgotten we were supposed to. Now, I'll have to find something. I have a red blouse that I never wear because it doesn't go with any of my other clothes. I dither about this, then make up my mind. Red jewelry. That's it, that's all: a coral necklace and earrings, a big ring carved in fish bone I bought in Cuba, and bracelets with red stones whose origin and material I have forgotten.

As for Adam, there's not much to choose from. He has no red clothes, just a red tie with little white hearts. I wonder who was making fun of him with a gift like that; I could swear it was Marta. It's fine for this evening. I help him put on some black pants and a light grey shirt. He loves the tie. He studies it closely while I tie it.

As soon as he's ready, though, he's gripped by fear. He's been asking me all day about the other guests. I've told him he'll know everyone, no need to panic, they're all friends, they all *know*. So what's the darned problem?

He sits on the sofa and watches while I move between the bathroom and the bedroom.

Does he realize this change in our twenty-year routine?

Adam was never ready on time. Being punctual was my obsession. We had to start getting ready very early, and I was always ready before him, regardless. I'd be the one sitting on the sofa waiting for him to finish shaving and fix his unruly hair. Postponed visits to the barber made this difficult, and the results were never very good. I used to tap the floor with my foot and leave the house in a state of irritation.

Adam doesn't show any sign of irritation, waiting on the couch.

Daniel and Marta carry the cast iron pot and help Adam negotiate their driveway, which is icier than ours. The cars I see on the street tell me we must be among the last to arrive.

They're all in the living room and the kitchen with a glass in hand, close to bowls of peanuts, pistachios, and pretzels. Adam smiles, which is the only way he knows to respond to their greetings. He was never very sociable. I'm happy he can now just pretend to be listening, which is what he always did, anyway.

Marta has set up tables in the basement, red tablecloths and napkins, small tablemats cut out in the shape of hearts, a plastic Eros at each setting.

We're hungry and soon sit down. Sauerkraut, mashed beans, salads, sausages, eggplant, rice with seafood, chicken curry. My liver and potatoes dish is a hit, and I'm glad I can still surprise them.

The men go upstairs to the living room, and the women stay on. Daniel insists Adam go with the men, in spite of the anxiety in his face. I nod my consent.

We talk about dieting. These women all have low-calorie recipes to share. This doesn't stop them wolfing down everything on the table, even as they calculate the calories in every bite. They're surprised I haven't yet switched to quinoa seeds, the new miracle food. I tell them my theory, which is that the human body doesn't necessarily know how to get the most out of unfamiliar foods. The others believe in alimentary diversity, I in nutritional history. No one agrees with me. They all carry on exchanging quinoa recipes. Lily's instructions on preparing all-saints'-worth essential oil is useful; this is a good moisturizer, especially for the hands, which get dry with age. She tells me about tea as a remedy for insomnia.

The cheese course reveals our greed again. I can't blame anyone for coming up with so many different varieties, since cheese certainly is part of our nutritional history. The sin, if there is a sin, is the number of pretzels everyone spreads with lashings of cheeses like *Frère Andre* and *La passion des anges*.

The next subject is the need to make a will. We discuss the pros and cons and analyze who should inherit more — the children or the husband — and in what proportion.

Dora wants to leave her fortune to her husband. She finds this ethical; they've worked together to build their fortune, and he has a right to take advantage of it. Children have to prove they deserve to be spoiled.

Sandra disagrees, saying it's foolish to give your husband everything, for that's like giving him a dowry for his next marriage.

Then there are our eternal remains. Roxana wants to be cremated, but a small cohort rebels against such a sinful thought: our Orthodox tradition wants us turned into land, not into ashes. Roxana doesn't care; she just doesn't want to freeze at forty below for six months every year. She has even talked about the acquisition of a small pigeonhole in a chapel not far from her place. Those who want to be buried have not yet started searching for the best spot. They're wavering between Montreal and Laval, between being far away or close to their kids and friends. Burial is not the main issue. The main question is, who would come and visit us?

Dora asks a disturbing question. "Do you realize we're going to start dying?"

We're young and lively, and, so far, we've mostly known happy events — birthday parties, weddings, and baptisms. When our parents died on the other side of the ocean, each of us went to the funerals and did our mourning over there.

I check on Adam. He's sitting in a corner of the living room with a glass of beer in his good hand. It looks as though he's listening carefully to what the others are saying, as he turns his head to every speaker. He sees me and thinks it's time to go. I signal to stay put. I know he's tired, but I want to stay a bit longer. I think the best strategy is to start drinking again, which I never used to do. Usually after the main course I drink only water, but water makes me sleepy and eager to get home.

The women are talking about dieting again. This is because the cakes have been brought out. Dessert is Marta's responsibility, and she spares no expense. There's cheesecake, chocolate mousse, and a flan. They all eat with gusto, amusing themselves with their own appetite. It's time to add up all the calories they've consumed in the course of the evening.

Marta and Daniel are leaving in a week for a holiday in Venezuela, on Margarita Island, with three of the other couples. They chose Chavez over his friend Fidel. People in our circle often take a week off in February and head south in a group. They speak about their last-minute preparations.

The talk moves to plucking and shaving and the amount of hair we still have on our pubis. Some say they're still hairy, others say they're, sadly, bald. Most are menopausal, so we share remedies for hot flashes. We're laughing and making fun of the shape, density and colour of our pubic hair when Daniel appears, looking for something. He hears laughter, catches a few words, and heads back upstairs.

As we say our goodnights, we realize that, for the first time, none of us danced at any point in the evening.

Adam never liked new foods much, and neither did I. However, he loved everything meaty, whereas I was always more interested in vegetables. I insisted on eating foods we ate as children and on avoiding everything that was not in season, like strawberries in winter and tomatoes in spring. Adam never agreed with me that this was against nature.

Our ancestors had no access to such variety year-round; they had to wait for warm weather to take advantage of the land's plenty. In the villages, those first sources of civilization, people ate what nature offered them, and, over the centuries, this became a ritual. Penury was transformed into tradition. Lent and Advent, for example: why did people fast then? Because there was no alternative.

In autumn, starting in November, the goats, mutton, and cows got pregnant and could not be milked anymore until spring, when they gave birth. Chickens laid fewer eggs in winter, too, sometimes none at all. The pig slaughter was postponed until the cold created a natural refrigerator. People had to feed themselves with what they had: carrots, potatoes, radishes, turnips, beans, peas, lentils, nuts, pickles and cabbage marinated in vinegar or brine. There were no fresh tomatoes, salad greens, asparagus, or cucumbers.

In early March, the chickens started to lay eggs and sit on them, and other livestock gave birth to lambs, calves, kids. Suddenly there was milk, cheese, and meat again; fields and gardens were bursting with new growth; fallow land was full of sorrel, rhubarb, nettles, amaranth, and patience. After the long months of making do with salted meat, lard, marinated vegetables, and dry seeds, the body cried out for the vitamins and minerals of fresh produce.

The summer was paradise for vegetables and fresh fruits. They were juicy, ripened out in the sun and not in warehouses, and chock-full of oxygen. First came the strawberries and cherries, and, later, the watermelons, apples, pears, and plums. In early June, people started with kidney beans and spring radishes. Then came the cucumbers and zucchini. By August, there were tomatoes, egg-plants, and peppers.

Summer meats were primarily chicken, duck, and goose. Some-times, there was game: rabbits and partridges from the harvested wheat fields. In some regions, there was fish.

And the cycle began again, year after year, without much variation.

Here, we have access to everything. Eating strawberries, toma-toes, and watermelon in winter is ungodly to me. Foregoing radish-es, turnips, marinated cabbage, and pickles seems to me a mortal sin.

Adam used to tease me about this with our guests, carefully ex-plaining how my seasonal interest had determined what they had on their plates. When he discovered an out-of-season ingredient, he pretended to be indignant.

"What is this horror? Why is this slice of tomato on my plate in the middle of winter? Who smuggled this forbidden product into our kitchen?"

I usually took this in good part, except when we were out shop-ping. He would be piling cucumbers and tomatoes into our shop-ping cart, and I radishes and zucchini. I used to take sadistic plea-sure in showing his out-of-season vegetables to him one week later, rotten in the refrigerator, before I threw them out in disdain.

As Adam so rarely cooked, he was obliged to eat what I put on his plate, and I had difficulty making a tomato salad in winter. I always preferred cabbage, or beets with a pinch of horseradish, or grated carrots and celery with salt and olive oil. I have occasionally gone so far as to try a parsley salad with garlic, fresh lemon juice, and extra-virgin olive oil. This last was a frequent cause of his sarcasm.

"Since when did your ancestors eat olive oil?"

To which I quickly replied, "You see how open-minded I am?"

More recently he had started to tease me about my new habit of adding a few drops of extra-virgin olive oil to a slice of Danish blue.

"No kidding. Danish blue! I bet your ancestors ate a lot of it, as their cheese was surely getting musty at the bottom of their barrel. If you want my opinion, though, the best way of helping you swallow that is to add onion. Take my shepherd's word for it."

Since he had his stroke, we've been eating what I like. My whole life I felt I had sacrificed my tastes for his: so much meat, of so many kinds, in so many different ways. If we could only calculate the number of animals that had been sacrificed on the altar of our kitchen. I had to put up with the smell of fried and boiled meat every day of the week.

Not any more. I can now devote myself to eggplants, tomatoes, marrows, radishes, and cabbages, all in their season. We eat light soups, mashed zucchini, barbecued eggplant, fruit compôtes. We have meat just once a week, on Sundays, and for holidays, and when we have guests.

Adam now eats whatever I prepare without any fuss, and he accepts my seasonal and heredity theories without a quibble. In the morning, he chews a few parsley leaves from the bunch set in a glass of water beside the coffee machine. He knows all about its vitamin content and its breath-freshening properties. Whatever I recommend, he accepts unquestioningly. He doesn't balk at marinated cabbage anymore, or ask for tomatoes in winter.

Is he happy about it?

I sometimes ask him if he likes my cooking. He says yes, with a large smile on his face. I don't ask for more. The beneficial effect on his health is obvious. His cholesterol dropped to the normal level without any help from Lipitor. I even stopped giving him Advil. His doctor had recommended the drug for his blood circulation, even though that was what had caused his cerebral vessels to break down. He is thin without being anaemic. His belly is supple, and his muscles are bulky.

If I have settled the matter of his body, I am still groping around for his brain. My genetic theories are not much help here, though the doctor did confirm that Adam's stroke can be traced back to his family history: two of his grandparents died from the same kind of stroke, but at the age of eighty.

Sometimes, I have a strange vision of his brain as a realm where a disconcerting enemy has settled. I see myself walking hand-in-hand with Adam in an immense forest. All around are centennial trees with their large trunks and magnificent crowns. Our goal is to get from one tree to another; we're looking for treasures buried beside their roots. What is slowing us down, though, is that the narrow paths through the forest are overgrown with weeds, ferns, and thorny branches. We try to cut through this thicket in order to move forward, but it closes in behind our every step. We move forward and backward, lose track of where we're headed, and end up retracing our steps.

This must be the maze of his mangled memory.

From time to time, I wonder at which moment we sign the blank cheque of our own destruction. What am I doing right now that will one day sentence me to death? What am I eating, drinking, and thinking that will do me in?

When was it that Adam took the path to a stroke? How did it happen that he ended up at odds with his own body? Why has he so readily given up battling his own genetic legacy?

Overprotected as we have become, our life is still in perpetual conflict with the world we live in, which is out to destroy us. Nature is not our friend, contrary to what some documentaries suggest about the beauty of the wilderness. Nature is ugly, hostile, brutal. It's only in tourist leaflets that it's beautiful. It was conceived to annihilate us with its cold, its heat, its wind, its rain, its heights, and its abysses.

It took us thousands and thousands of years to tame it, to convince it to accept our presence. We deciphered the secret of its edible fruits and its poisonous ones, we dug up its roots, we hiked in its forests to pick its bounty, and we learned to heal our wounds with its most humble weeds. We have become a race of vanguards and destroyers.

The malediction, however, remains in our blood. We transfer it to our kind from generation to generation. We are not programmed to last. We are doomed from the day we are born.

On Monday, March 6th, the temperature goes up to minus nine. In the morning, I go out onto the balcony to watch two squirrels chasing each other up and down the trunk of the maple tree. At dawn, I had the impression I heard birds singing.

Adam follows me, dragging his feet in his slippers. He doesn't look good. Nothing I say seems to interest him. He's turned in on himself. I know this from his eyes, which avoid mine.

There's no point in asking him what he's thinking about. For a while, I did put this question to him, and he soon learned to take this as a test and be wary. He was afraid of getting the answer wrong.

Odd that he's ashamed of his own imperfections and still unable to touch the nature of his condition. What happened to him? What did he do? He's unable to figure it out; he's just waiting for an explanation. As long as I give no clear account, he prefers to keep quiet. Until the elucidation of the mystery, he carefully avoids discussion.

I'm going to barbecue today. I defrost two steaks and light the coals. We could say we're celebrating the early spring, if we really need a reason for eating meat.

I ask Adam if he wants to watch the grill, sprinkle the coals from time to time, turn the steaks over, but he says no. He doesn't like playing with fire. The fierce light and the heat of the incandescent ashes frighten him. Perhaps the fire illuminates something dark in his brain, some well-buried tragedies. In the mysterious forest of his brain, I'm sure there's a trunk with some horrible secrets lurking somewhere in the mud of the past.

I don't know if these memories are related to his own experience or to that of previous generations of hunters, warriors, and murderers. If he doesn't find recent memories of his own, perhaps he unearths the big fires lit by Genghis Khan in Asia or by the Ottomans at the siege of Vienna, the cruelties of the Crusaders in the magnificent city of Constantinople, or the torching of the Temple in Jerusalem.

We have our checkup tomorrow. This is the least busy day of Sara's week. Apparently, people just don't go to the dentist on Tuesdays. She called us in for the end of the day so she can spend a little more time with us. This is also the only way to avoid some of our acquaintances who don't know about Adam's accident and who might ask questions in front of other patients. She even wants to send her receptionist and one of the assistants home.

On our arrival, Sara is busy with an emergency – a young man with an abscess. It takes longer than usual, and Katy, the assistant to the other dentist, who is on holiday, is getting impatient. She was expecting to leave early, but she cannot go until Sara says the word.

Adam takes a seat in the waiting room. He looks exhausted and is shaking slightly, the way he does when I take him to the doctor. It's no good explaining that this is Sara's office, our daughter's. He should remember he helped her with the renovations when she bought the dental practice. That was the last time he helped her out. He changed the carpet and took down the wall between the receptionist's office and the waiting room.

Tina, Sara's assistant, asks me to go with her for an X-ray. Adam asks if he can come with me. I reassure him I won't be long and try to convince him to flip through one of the women's magazines on the small table.

Tina does not look happy, either. Her cheeks are red, whether

from anger or fatigue. Sometimes, Sara has told me, there are con-
flicts between the two assistants.

When I come back to the waiting room, Adam is standing at the
window watching cars in the street. It's already dark, and the traffic
has started to slow down.

Sara leads us into her office. She always starts with me, in order
to reassure Adam, who keeps us company on a little stool in the
corner. My instinct was right: Katy has done practically nothing
all day. Because Katy is not herself on holiday, she was supposed
to help Tina, sterilize all the instruments, call some patients, and
settle the bill from the insurance company, but all she has done is
surf the Web.

Tina says nothing, but she's handling the suction tube pretty
briskly.

I feel a bit guilty about her. Does Sara realize that, while Katy
and the receptionist have now gone home, Tina is working overtime because of us?

My teeth are giving up on me, one by one. My crowns are wearing out, and some deep pockets have formed in the gums where
food collects and gets infected, despite the tools Sara has given
me. This evening, she discovers another pocket at the back of my
mouth and she cleans this out. I can see blood all along the suction
tube. She penetrates deeper and deeper, asking me if it hurts. I say
no. Tina laughs skeptically, but Sara reassures her:

"She's the only one who can stand this without an anaesthetic."

I tell myself this is for my own good.

When it's Adam's turn, she has to freeze him, otherwise she
fears hurting him when she does the cleaning. The last time, he
reacted rather well, but she does not want to risk it. His acidic saliva
means tartar under the gum, and she needs the curette for that.

Sara tells me the details while showing me the inside of his mouth on her little mirror. Adam needs an implant, but what's most urgent is a night-guard to stop him from grinding his teeth and wearing away the enamel. When Tina goes out to check on her sterilizing machine, I take charge of the suction of the blood from Adam's gums.

"Your blue blood, Daddy," says Sara playfully.

Adam does not seem amused. Since the stroke, I have never joked about his aristocratic background, with all those philosophers and professors in the family.

When we're done, Sara asks if I can give her a lift home. She comes to work by bus, as she lives in the neighbourhood, but the trip home is tiresome, and Michael usually drives her home. This evening she's given him a break.

Once we get there, she invites us in for a drink, but it's already late and we go on our way. She kisses us goodbye and jumps out of the car.

This weekend, I want to finish Salman Rushdie's *Luka and the Fire of Life,* even though the large cast of characters is dizzying. For a children's book, I find it a little overcharged.

Next to me in bed, Adam flips through a cartoon book. He looks up from time to time to watch me reading. I don't say anything.

On page fifty-four, I come across a passage that makes me laugh. It is the riddle competition between Luka and The Old Man of the River. I ask Adam if he wants to listen to the riddles in English. He is happy with this. His own book is clearly of no great interest.

I start with this one: "It stands on one leg with its heart in its head."

Adam laughs. I ask him why.

"Because that's too difficult for me."

I start laughing, as well. It's too difficult for me, too.

I tell him the answer in English: a cabbage. But he doesn't remember the word. I tell him the answer in Romanian: *varza*.

For a few seconds, I hoped he would react with the same jokes over the Dace origin of our language, but not this time.

"Don't you remember, Adam? *Mazare, varza, viezure, miez, zmeura*" – peas, cabbage, badger, crumb, raspberry –"those are words in Dace, the language we were speaking before the Roman conquest of Dacia, our mythical mother country."

Linguists have established a list of the Dace words in modern Romanian, and most of them include the letter z.

Adam completely forgot the reply he once gave me when I served him peas: "Where are the *varza, viezure, miez, zmeura?*"

Another thing he does not remember is the conversation we used to have over the origin of the Romanian words for *pizda* – cunt – and *pula* – cock. He was explaining that *pizda* was probably Dace; the proof was either the presence of the letter z or its similarity to the Dace word for the smelly cheese, *branza*. *Pula,* on the other hand, could not be anything other than Latin, considering how similar the word is to apulum. He insisted on this, though I told him *apulum* has nothing to do with *pula; it* means a fortress or settlement.

"As you can see, we've been fucked ever since the dawn of time," Adam concluded.

We could have simply checked their origin in the Romanian dictionary, DEX, that we brought with us in our baggage. But why dissipate the magic of Adam's etymology lessons?

"What is it that you can keep after giving it to someone else?"

"This one's is too difficult, too," says Adam.

His eyes show increasing worry. What if the answer is in fact very simple and he should have known the answer?

I reassure him. "Indian wisdom, what can I say? For me it is as difficult as it is for you. The answer is, 'Your word.'"

He doesn't get it.

"It means that you can give your word, but you keep it at the same time," I say, not sure this is right.

"You mean that I, too – I have to keep my word after giving it?"

"I don't know," I admitted. "Do you still want to listen to some other riddles?

He reluctantly says yes. I tell him that from now on I will give him the answer as well, so he won't have to guess:

"This is really funny, listen: 'What do sea monsters eat? Fish and ships.'"

Adam does not find it funny.

"Do you not remember our trip to the Atlantic Provinces? In Halifax, we ate fish and chips and drank Alexander Keith's beer. Fish and chips. Here, instead of chips they say ships."

"When did we go to Halifax?" Adam asks, not paying any attention to my explanation.

"For your forty-fifth birthday. We toured the Atlantic provinces by car, three thousand kilometers in fifteen days. You drove, as I had my foot in a cast."

"Do we have pictures?"

"Unfortunately not. We lost the camera's memory card. There are no pictures from that trip."

The lack of proof makes Adam suspicious. It isn't the first time he thinks I may be messing with his memories. He says he doesn't remember anything.

"It doesn't matter," I tell him. I want to continue reading my book. I already regret getting him into this English lesson. "Listen to this one, it's very cute: 'What has been there for millions of years but is never more than a month old?' The answer is, the moon."

I laugh. I want him to understand it's witty. But Adam is difficult to convince.

"Would you have guessed the answer?" he asks me hesitantly.

"No, not at all. It isn't easy. But it is witty, you have to admit."

Adam agrees, but he does not find it funny at all.

I tell him that's it, even though there are some other riddles. Riddles may not be the best way to practise a foreign language.

What disappoints me is not so much that he has lost his English as that he has lost his sense of humour.

Over the next week, the temperature reaches twenty-five degrees. Some meteorologists say this is the warmest winter in the past six-ty-five years. Birds have already started to return. Almost every day I see flocks of ducks and geese flying north. In *Maclean's*, I read that the majority of robins did not even leave the country. In the morn-ing, I hear them singing, lined up like pearls on the electric wires. I also read that mammals and amphibians are coming out of hiberna-tion sooner, while some never hibernated at all. The worst thing is that pests have not been killed by the cold over the winter, as they usually are: corn flea beetles, bean leaf beetles, and pine beetles will ravage crops and trees. Blackflies, ticks, hornets, and wasps may plague us as never before. Grass fires will ravage the Prairies even before the arrival of spring.

This mild weather threatens what some analysts call our sense of self. Simply put, the change in the climate will alter our Ca-nadian identity. Winter isn't just the season when people put on snow-pants, tuques, and Kanuk coats; winter is what makes the dif-ference between us and the rest of the world. The freezing cold has been the pride of Canadians, something no one could take away from us. In what ways will the Canadian identity change without this harsh season?

Defying winter was always the final ordeal a newcomer had to face in becoming a Canadian. Winter was the immigrant's baptism. It was a natural border that kept the unwanted out, and we would now have to watch out for barbarous hordes invading the country.

The myths surrounding the Canadian winter would melt as readily as the polar cap.

The article ends on a sober note about the impossibility of there ever being another Wayne Gretzky if the backyard skating rink where he played as a kid disappeared forever.

I take the garden chairs out on to the patio so that Adam can sun-bathe while I'm at school. At eight o'clock, the temperature is al-ready so mild that he can wear just a T-shirt.

Before leaving, I repeat to Adam that today I won't be back until ten o'clock because of parent-teacher meetings to discuss the second term report. I explain to him once again that he should eat the eggplant stew I've left on the counter. He can eat it without heating it in the microwave; I'm not comfortable with the idea of him turning on any appliance other than the TV.

I finish school at four o'clock, but am too tired to make the trip home twice. I prefer to stay at school till seven o'clock, when the meetings begin. I check my email, flip through a magazine, and start marking a grammar test. Mario invites me to go out to eat in the neighbourhood, but I decline, saying I brought a double lunch. I always keep a Tupperware container full of nuts in my drawer, too. I crunch some pistachios as I go over the tests.

Robert comes to get his bag. I pull my chair towards the desk to let him through to his, but I don't speak to him. I thought he would leave soon, as usual, but he sits down, and searches for something in his drawer. He has just gotten back from Italy, where he went to celebrate his daughter's birthday. On his return, I asked him if he had had a good trip, but nothing further. I want to avoid contact with him, as I don't like his attitude.

Sometimes I think I'm too cautious. Since I am the wife of a sick man, I may be too sensitive to people's attitudes towards me. As I feel weaker than before, I feel people treat me as though I'm pitiful. I never feel this more intensely than with Robert.

Mario stayed at school, too, in the end. He got himself a large coffee from the machine and withdrew to his desk behind a pile of papers. I see him flipping through them without enthusiasm. To our left, Yves, the math teacher, is talking loudly, as usual. We hear his voice on the far side of the staff room. He's talking politics about the student strike.

Most of our colleagues either went out to eat or went home. They start coming back by 6.30.

The meetings with the parents take place in the school gym, as usual. For an hour or so, we can hear the three janitors putting out the tables for the teachers and chairs for the parents.

I run into the building manager, Philippe, in the corridor and stop to chat. We're old acquaintances; he worked at Saint Norbert when I was teaching there, a few years ago. Last autumn, I discovered him here. Today, for the first time, I ask why he left Saint Norbert. He tells me there was too much bureaucracy over there. I said I understand, but I cannot figure out in which way the School Board red tape could possibly affect his work.

Philippe looks like an old rocker, with his white hair pulled into a ponytail, his battered jeans, and his turtleneck. A down-market Steve Jobs. He smells, even from afar, of cigarettes. From my second floor classroom window I sometimes see him smoking in the backyard. When we were at Saint Norbert, he was still living with his mother, who has since died of cancer.

At seven o'clock, when I go down into the gymnasium, the five rows of chairs in front of my table are already occupied. Among the parents I specifically asked to come, only Jamal's and Ernesto's have shown up. Sabrina's mother has avoided me since our last conversation over the phone. I regularly send her messages through Sabrina's agenda, but she never signs them, which further complicates my life. She has abandoned the fight for her daughter, and she would like me to do the same and leave her alone. Her cell phone is always turned off, and the answering machine never works at home. I had to mail her a letter in order to ask her to come to this meeting. Recently, Sabrina was suspended for two weeks. I'm not even sure her mother knew. A few days after Sabrina's return, the principal suspends her again, this time for scratching Moses's cheeks during recess.

Jamal's parents look like teenagers. The father is Haitian and the mother Moroccan. Jamal inherited his father's curly hair and his mother's magnificent eyes. They've brought their other three children with them, toddlers now racing around the gym. I imagine how difficult it must be for them to put up with each other in order to be here and face every teacher in the room. I've been told they're divorced, and Jamal is commuting every week between two houses and is not very welcome in either.

"What can we do for Jamal?" they ask me.

Do they know that for their son, school is nothing other than a boring waiting room until September, when he'll be old enough to drop out? And that he's decided, in the meantime, to cause as much trouble as possible in every class?

They are both aware of this. Nevertheless, the father says that at home, Jamal is quiet and polite. I answer that this is the case with all disruptive students. At home they are all angels. The mother promises to hire a private tutor for Jamal. She asks if I could give him some supplementary work. I tell her that what he has in the book, which he hasn't opened all term, will be enough. I promise her, though, to photocopy some extra exercises for him. She also asks me to make a note of incidents in his agenda, but Jamal pretends he's lost it. She promises to buy a new one. Too many promises all at once. Otherwise, they're the same old promises she made to me last term.

Next in line is Ernesto's mother, who turns heads with her mini-skirt and décolletage. She wears heavy makeup and a blond wig that's all wrong with her Colombian olive skin.

She repeats the same things she says over the phone, that she's lost control over her son since the death of her mother, who was taking care of him. Ernesto has been at war with his mother ever since. She promises to ask for her ex-husband's help as soon as she tracks him down.

By nine o'clock, Selena's parents are the only ones I still have to see. This is the first time I've met this couple, and I wonder why they're here. Selena is not terribly smart, but at least she's quiet. Her mother is Mexican and her father Asian, I don't know where from.

They're here to ask for the same psychological support for Selena that her big sister gets. I don't know what they're talking about. The mother tells me she recently learned she has cancer, and the school decided to support the older girl, who is in the ninth grade. They do not understand why Selena was excluded, as she needs help just as much as her sister. She smiles, but her husband looks at me with frowning eyes. I note the request and promise to speak to the principal about it.

The gym is almost empty. There were fewer people than usual, probably because of the hot weather. Only Tasha, the science teacher, still has a number of parents waiting. Because of her French (she was born in Russia), her explanations take a long time. What I don't understand is why she insists on going over the whole report card, which the parents already got by mail.

In the far corner, I see Oliver, the art teacher, who is already done, in spite of the scolding he gave the parents for their untalented children. He is walking from table to table to stretch his good leg, leaning on his cane, and he has finally found a reason for dissatisfaction: the water bottles. This year, the principal left them at the entrance to the gym for teachers to help themselves. Last year some of the seventh graders walked around to our tables with a basket full of the bottles. Oliver notes this decline in service in his agenda for the next General Assembly.

This morning, before the start of classes, he came to my corner to lecture me. This is not the first time he has told me he hates my students. My group nine, with students like Sabrina, Ernesto, and Jamal, has the reputation of disrupting every class – especially art class. I tell him I'm powerless as I'm their tutor, not their mother. He carried on, telling me that Ernesto had scribbled something porno-graphic on his desk, Jamal drew the Haitian flag on his art outfit, and Sabrina threw a pot of red ink on Marc's drawings. And they all left without cleaning their tools. I promise to do my best to calm them down. I don't dare give Oliver the same advice I give some of the other teachers, that it is better to interest them than to threaten them.

By lunchtime, his mood had completely changed. He came over to show me a picture he found on the Internet. It was an image taken at the beginning of the century, of the spot where our school was to be built, with the church on the other side of the street and some carts parked in front of it. At that time, Saint Justin School was noth-ing more than a wasteland. There was a white house with carved pillars nearby, and Oliver pointed out an old woman sitting on the balcony. She looked like she was waiting for somebody to come down St. Justin Street. This house today is a ruin that nobody wants.

I pretended to be enthusiastic about his discovery. I was relieved it was just a picture and nothing more serious. The day before, Oli-ver was in the staff room with a notice he had ripped off the bath-room wall with instructions for hand washing. Were we that stupid that we had to be told how to wet, soap, scrub, and rinse our hands? Who took us for such brainless creatures? He wanted to take this complaint to the top.

I'm home by ten o'clock. The light in the living room is on, the TV is blaring, and Adam is asleep on the couch. He doesn't hear the front door and he doesn't hear my footsteps on the stairs.

I watch him sleeping, his palms together under his left cheek. At this moment, he looks the same to me – the man I have watched sleeping all these years. There's nothing to suggest he has changed. His body, his face, his lips are the same. This is the man I fell in love with. The small stain on his brain cannot turn him into someone else, someone less worthy of being loved, someone who deserves to be abandoned.

Who could I replace him with? With Oliver, who displays his cane like a trophy to show me he is a better choice, despite his stiff leg? With Robert, who pretends to be disturbed by my chair? Or with Mario, divorced, who is forever working on a Master's, always preoccupied by his children's problems?

On Friday evening, Adam chews his olives bitterly. The intact quarter of his brain has not forgotten to hate the Mediterranean diet. The most difficult thing for me is to convince him that olives are part of our own heritage, sort of. That terrible heritage. He always hated this topic, which used to come up in many of our conversations.

"There are no olive trees at home, it's as simple as that," he always said.

This was how he tried to stop stocking such products in our refrigerator. Not to mention the extra-virgin olive oil. What a nightmare to discover that in a salad.

"My body does not know how to digest it, according to your theory, as I did not eat it when I was child. So why do you want to kill me with this poison? It tastes bitter, too."

"The Bible says we also have to put bitter things in our mouth."

"Can you please show me that passage in the Bible? If so, I will eat it, binding included."

This was the kind of exchange we used to have on evenings when I didn't have time to cook and improvised with a simple meal that was not to Adam's taste.

I was just as insistent as he was. I was tireless in explaining my theory to him on the place of olives in our national cuisine.

We did not have olive trees because of the climate, that's true, but we did have the Greeks. And during their hundred-year reign, they surely brought olives with them. Olives are easily kept in brine. The leaders of our Orthodox church were often Greek, and I was certain they must have introduced some of the foods they used to eat. My parents were crazy about olives. This was not the case in Adam's family, and the only way I could explain that was that his ancestors came from an isolated mountainous region.

Adam doesn't object to olives any more, but he still doesn't like them. He chews them unwillingly, convinced I've told him they're good for him. Which is a reason that trumps all others.

On Sunday morning, I tell him about a *Maclean's* article on the economics and demographics of the new Canada. For the first time since Confederation, wealth is concentrated in the West. The only consolation, if we need one, is that the West is also suffering from what economists call the Dutch disease, by which they mean an overreliance on the export of raw materials.

"You were a Liberal, Adam," I add. "You wanted to join the Liberal party in order to fix it. The Grits needed you after two university professors ruined the party. It was time for an immigrant engineer to put their big train back on the rails."

Adam laughs, which pleases me. It seems that the political fibber is still there. I laugh, too, and arrange his hair, which is standing up in a comical comb that makes him look like Tintin.

"The Conservatives were lucky this time. And look at the result. They're forcing me to keep on working until I'm seventy years old."

The phone rings. It's Sara saying goodbye before leaving for a cruise. George is driving them to Plattsburg, and then they're catching a flight to Florida. I renew my offer to pick them up at the airport when they get back next week, but Sara declines. Michael's father will make the trip again, mainly because they're getting in at midnight.

Adam looks at me dazed. He waits for some explanation. He pays unusual attention when I speak to Sara.

"They're going on a Caribbean cruise," I tell him. "They'll eat lots of junk food and lie on a chaise-longue in the sun all day, connected to a straw."

The children are well aware of my opinion of such vacations. This is why they waited until the last minute to tell me about their departure.

This gives me an idea, though. Adam and I will stay in their apartment for the weekend, just for a change.

Adam agrees on the spot. Yet as soon as I start packing, his cheerfulness vanishes. Where are we going with all that baggage?

I don't have time to sit down with him and explain it all again. I run from one room to another, tossing items we will need into a bag: pyjamas, shoes, toothbrushes, pills.

Adam sits on the sofa, his head bent downwards. Does he believe this is a scheme to oust him? Does he fear banishment to a rest home?

"We're going to Sara's," I finally reassure him.

"But why?"

"To be downtown."

Ah, this matter of being downtown. Finally, I do not want that any longer. After years of hating suburbia, I have finally grown to like it. And the fact that I have finally found a job near my house is a heavenly gift.

We get to the apartment on Ridgewood by noon.

I like this street. We bought this apartment close to the Université de Montréal when Sara was still a student, but she didn't really take advantage of being there. It was only a twenty-minute walk, but she rarely walked. Michael gave her a lift, most of the time, up the mountain to the Faculty of Dentistry, on his way to the hospital where he was doing his residency. In winter, she even preferred to be there an hour early just to avoid getting there in a sweat.

They're still living here, even after graduating. At first, they found it too small, but now they're used to it. They appreciate the interior parking for Michael's car and the bus out front that Sara takes to work. They have no kids yet, and they're not too keen to buy a house and get into debt.

I dream about the day when I will move into this apartment. We bought it for our old age when we would not be able to run a house. Adam insisted on doing it during the subprime crisis, when few people were investing in real estate. We were also able to take advantage of the lowest interest rates in history. This is how we found ourselves with a second mortgage, but it wasn't too much of a sacrifice as our house is now paid for.

The kids are now in charge of paying the expenses. I stopped paying the mortgage after Adam's stroke, I needed the money to keep our own household going.

Sara has kept the bright colours we chose when we bought the apartment: red and orange. The rooms still smells new, too, as they're always buying furniture. Their last acquisition was a white leather couch. This horrid leather. They bought it on the sly, as they know my opinion of leather: cold in winter, sticky in summer. I dream of the day I can dump my own leather sofas. I only keep them for sentimental reasons, which is always a bad idea. When I told the kids I wanted to replace them with new, fabric-covered sofas, Sara said that Adam loved the leather ones. It's true; we bought them when we got our first permanent jobs here. This was proof of our success, and it had given us a feeling of security.

We settle in their office, where Sara has a sofa bed, also black leather. On the walls, Sara has added two new paintings of white lilacs on a violet background. From time to time she still paints. This was the passion of her childhood, when she wanted to enroll in art school. Behind the door, she keeps the easel with a half-finished painting of grey skyscrapers on a foggy morning.

Whenever I'm alone in their apartment, I check out Sara's new dresses, skirts, and blouses. My mother used to do this with my things, so I find nothing wrong with it. Unlike my mother, who used to wear the clothes I no longer wanted, I can't wear anything of Sara's. Our tastes are completely different.

What surprises me is how tidy Sara has become. When she lived at home, her room was a mess. Her underwear was higgelty-piggelty in one messy drawer, and her blouses and T-shirts were in a pile on the chair and on her bed. She had to be ordered to clean up her room.

Now, her blouses are all on hangers, her pullovers are folded, her underclothes are arranged neatly in separate drawers. Her shoes are nicely lined up, too, with steel shoetrees stretching the leather.

I ask Adam to turn on the TV while I get organized in the kitchen. He can't work the remote control, and it takes me a few minutes to figure it out myself.

Sara is accumulating sophisticated kitchenware – coffee mugs, platters, ladles, jars – all from the most expensive stores. A potted plant looks as though it hasn't been watered for some time. I decide to save it even though I did not actually intend to tell Sara about this invasion.

The children don't cook much, so their fridge is full of jars, pickles, jams, cheeses, and sausages. I will have to confess to staying here, for sure, as I've already opened most of the jars to taste the marinated seafood, almond-stuffed olives, Greek feta in olive oil and basil leaves, and sour cherry compote.

Sara loves the same things I love, and when she does cook she makes dishes she learned from me.

I make a platter of cold cuts and open a bottle of wine. Adam is excited. How come he remembers that he likes this kind of sausage?

He eats with gusto and drinks deeply. I'm afraid he'll have a headache later, so I give him Advil right away. After all, we're on vacation.

At naptime, he stays in the living room to watch TV. Sara has more channels than we do, and he treats himself to his wildlife documentaries.

I try to snooze. It's warm and comfortable, and I'm tired, but I can't fall asleep. The pianist who lives on the fourth floor has just started her afternoon practice. I recognize the tune, which is one that Sara used to sing to me. Unable to fall asleep, I hum the notes the pianist is playing over and over again, and this calms me.

An hour later, I ask Adam if he wants to take a walk. He says yes, his eyes on the screen.

We walk down Ridgewood to Côte-des-Neiges, then over to Queen Mary. We stop in at the bookstore, Olivieri, and then sit down for coffee and cake outside the Brûlerie Saint-Denis.

The terrace is crowded with students exhausted after a demonstration downtown. They're striking against the tuition fee hike announced by Charest's Liberal government. It's cold, but they've taken their coats off. Adam and I took the last available table.

Many of them are smoking. I feel like a cigarette, too, but I don't feel like getting up to find a place to buy them. I know there's a *dépanneur* nearby, but I don't have the energy to go. When I stopped smoking, it was because it was a nuisance having to buy them.

Somebody stops at the railing. It's Victor, of course. He's an artist friend who lives nearby, and he has a way of showing up any time one of us stops for coffee around here. He has some special radar beamed on Côte-des-Neiges cafés.

I invite him to join us, but he says he's busy. I know what that means. It means he'll now describe all his projects, which could take hours. I'm right. He's leaning on the railing, lecturing us about his new work. The students don't like him talking in a language they don't know.

Adam doesn't remember Victor, and I think he finds Victor's

71

long, bushy beard and his white ponytail alarming. I can't help him right now, for Victor doesn't know much about Adam's condition. He just thinks Adam's a bit crazy, but then Victor takes a dark view of everything.

By four o'clock, the sun has gone behind the buildings on the other side of the street, and the temperature is dropping. We're shivering, and the students are chilled, too, but they're not ready to leave yet. They're sure they'll win against the Liberals, and this warms their blood.

We head back to Sara's, which takes longer than I thought, for Adam has trouble getting up the hill. We find a bench and sit down to let him catch his breath.

The street is always busy, close to the university, full of student lodgings, and it's the time of day when they're walking their dogs and running errands. They walk effortlessly, and we watch them with envy.

We're close to the place where I crashed my car, I realize.

"Do you remember the accident, Adam?"

"What accident?"

"The fender-bender with the young woman." I point at the spot, on the curb behind us.

"I'm not sure," he says. "Was that a long time ago?"

"Almost five years."

"I don't really remember."

It happened a few months after we bought the apartment. We took our time renovating the bathroom and the kitchen. It was late afternoon, already dark, and I was coming to take window measurements so I could order curtains, driving carelessly on this zigzagging street, where there's no street parking. I wasn't going more than the speed limit, but I was distracted by the rents advertised on a new building to my left, which is how it happened. I had noticed

72

the car ahead, but thought it was moving. I crushed its bumper and suffered worse damage to my own car, a broken light, a bent hood, and a cracked radiator. When I saw orange liquid spilling on to the asphalt, I thought it was my own blood.

Behind the wheel was a young woman who had forgotten to turn on her lights and who had stopped in the street to look for an address,

She got out of the car and yelled at me. "*Merde*, I've just had it fixed!"

She was expecting a violent reaction from me and was making the first move. But I didn't argue. This was my first accident. It happened because of her, but it was mainly my fault. I told her to calm down as I would to pay for the repairs.

It was the end of November and very cold. I invited her inside my car to talk. I asked for her cell phone to call my husband.

I told Adam what had happened. He told me not to do anything for the moment, just to turn on my indicators, if they were still working. He'd be there as soon as he could.

While we waited, the young woman told me she lived in a flat on Côte-des-Neiges and was graduating from law school next year. She lived alone and was doing her best, but everything was always going wrong. It was then that she said, "You're lucky to have someone to call at a time like this."

When Adam got there, he checked my knees to see how badly I was hurt. Then he called Stavros from his cellphone and asked if he could replace a bumper without going through the insurance company. He told the young woman everything was fine. She should go to our garage to get it fixed, and he would pay the bill.

The repairs to her Volvo cost us $1,500, but my Toyota was finished. Stavros wanted $4,000 to fix it, but Adam preferred to buy another car. That's the one I'm driving now, a black Nissan.

This evening, we eat more sausage and cheese and drink beer. The kids throw a lot of parties, and there are impressive quantities of alcohol in their apartment.

I want to go to bed early, and Adam has to come with me, as I'm not sure he knows how to turn things off here. I'm obsessed that nothing be left on overnight.

The next morning, we take the bus to Alexis Nihon, where I restock my supply of henna at Pharmaprix. Adam sits on a bench while I shop, and we have lunch at a small restaurant before going back to Sara's. Adam settles down in front of the TV, but I tell him we have to go home. I have to do my cooking for the week.

I clean up, water Sara's plant one more time, and take out the garbage.

It's Easter, six days of leisure I don't yet know what to do with. I giggle at Adam, who is rolling around in bed like a kitten.

I adore Adam's body. I love him even more than I did when we were young. Despite the new hormones of misfortune that he is now releasing, he has kept his shape and, most of all, his smell. He's still my man.

When we go to bed, he faces me, puts his good arm around my neck, and I rest my head on his shoulder. I slip my fingers between the buttons of his pyjamas and rub his belly. After a quarter of an hour, though, I get him to turn over, as he will soon start snoring. In the night, I put one arm around his waist, the other on his head. When I'm awake, I tap him gently, and he responds by tapping my hand tenderly or by rubbing my feet with his instep. There is a mute language between our two bodies, which have known each other for such a long time.

I also like to caress his penis through the soft fabric of his pyjamas. I've always done this, but it isn't the invitation to have sex that it used to be. It's just a declaration of ownership, my taking possession of his body. Adam is mine. The blot on his brain doesn't diminish the fact that his body is a perfect engine, beyond understanding. Adam is not just a collection of short-circuited neurons. He's a fortress of muscles, veins, and organs that pulse, beat, and pound. Nothing can annihilate this complex scaffolding, which stands and acts by itself. I think this is a miracle.

I tell Adam about Loïc, my student from group nine. He has been diagnosed with attention deficit hyperactivity disorder and he has no friends. No one in his class speaks to him, except to ask him for a pencil, an eraser, or liquid paper. His mother makes sure he always has some, for he always misplaces things, if he hasn't forgotten his pencil case altogether. He wears braces and the elastics loosen by the end of the day. When he speaks, he opens his mouth like a fish to touch them with his tongue.

He sometimes comes to my classroom at lunchtime to chat. On Friday, he told me about his plan to register at *l'Ecole de l'humour* to become a stand-up comedian. I asked him if, when he became famous, he would still remember his French teacher and give me an autograph. He said of course. He even intended to do a gag about my way of saying, "I am non-negotiable" whenever they ask me to give them a break with so much homework. I asked him if this was a kind of inside joke and he said, yes, they all make fun of me at recess, mimicking the way I say that.

Loïc has the memory of an elephant, and I'm convinced he's been misdiagnosed. I confide in him the line is a quote from Robert Lepage's movie *The Hidden Face of the Moon*.

As for his autograph, Loïc tells me I'd get one, for sure. He has already worked out his artist signature. I ask him to show me, and he signs his name on the first page of my agenda.

At lunchtime, I show Adam Loïc's signature, and he asks if he can put his own next to it. I agree. He has forgotten the baroque signature he used to use. He used to say this was a way of making sure crooks couldn't forge his signature, but I knew it was pure narcissism. Using his left hand, he now has difficulty just writing his name.

I have always told him about my day, about how my students astonish me. I'm still impressed by their spontaneity; blown away by their willingness to defy the system, to escape, slip through our fingers. Adults always seem to be out to get them. Their books and movies depict grown-ups as the problem and children as saviours. They're good at mixing lies and truth, and they're remorseless.

At school, we have many ways of punishing the insubordinate. There are piles of papers in the secretary's office, all waiting to be filled in, signed, and countersigned by teachers, specialists, the principal, parents. Rebels move through all the levels of Purgatory. They're quick to apologize and pretend they're sorry when the truth is, they feel not the slightest remorse. They know they're right, and they hate grown-ups for wanting to make them feel wrong.

The doctors have tried to convince me that Adam has regressed to his childhood, but I know they're mistaken. Tormented though he is, my husband is still an adult. His baffled memory has not forgotten the height of the obstacles standing between an individual and the world, and he's still aware of the consequences of what he does.

What of the future?

For his young counterparts at Saint Justin, the future is dark, overshadowed by climate change, which will transform the human being into a savage beast. My students are fired by the need for justice in a world that has lost its bearings.

Adam has simply stopped thinking about the future, even about tomorrow. He lives in a perpetual present that's only slightly darkened by the shadow of yesterday. He can take full advantage of what each moment has to offer.

Will he ever recover? Will he ever regain what he once knew? And what would be the point? To rebuild his career, educate his child, serve society? What for, when all he wants is peace?

I envy him for so brazenly escaping the system. He refused to play the game.

Today, my first day off, I will embark on my criminal plan to cut down half of the lilacs in the garden, the ones that encroach on the grapevines. Adam made the trellis for the vines, promising me shade on the patio all summer, and though I was skeptical about getting any grapes from our own vineyard, it actually worked. Some years, we get such a bumper crop we can even make juice. The vines are much less plentiful on the side with the lilacs. I think they know I don't like them and have declared war. In springtime, the flowers are anaemic and last only a day or two, but the leaves stay green until late in the autumn. I often asked Adam to cut them back.

He was against this. He just didn't like the idea of cutting down trees. The garden now looks like fallow land because of all the flowers Adam planted there over the years. There was no way to convince him to reduce the undergrowth of daisies, lilies, gentians, hyacinths, roses, freesia, phlox, sweet peas, mulberry and black-berry bushes.

We go outside, where the grass is already getting green. I should rake the last of the fall leaves. We're wearing tuques, gloves, and old winter coats. The day is cold and dark, as dark as my intentions. This is the day I'll sacrifice the lamb.

I take out the handsaw from the hut and tell Adam to follow me. I show him the lilac branches I want to cut down. He asks me how he can help. I tell him to hold them steady while I saw them down to their roots.

I'm good at this kind of work, but I'm not really strong enough for it. The effort exhausts me, but I do manage to clear the lilacs.

Adam carries the cut branches onto the stone platform into the middle of the backyard. In summer, we set up a small table here close to the grill.

I study the grapevines I have now liberated from their hos-tile neighbour. Each spring, I take pictures and send them to my brother-in-law, in the countryside back home, to show them to my father-in-law. The old man takes his time analyzing them, draw-ing arrows, and writing down detailed instructions on how best to prune them. This year, he told me I had to cut down all the old vines to let the young ones grow, as they're the ones that bear the fruit. I'll probably have less shade this year, but I should have a good crop.

That's it for today. I was thinking of calling Michael to help me take down the car shelter, but I don't feel like it now. Our Armenian neighbours from across the street are having trouble with theirs. They don't see eye to eye on how to get the fabric off the structure. After a few unsuccessful attempts, the man decides to do it his way, and his wife leaves him to it and starts weeding the flowerbeds instead. I spy on them for a bit from behind the curtain of my office window until he asks for her help with the structure itself.

What next? I'll help Adam with his French and English vocabulary. Then we'll spend an hour on his handwriting. He wastes time going for the crayon with his left hand, imploring me with his eyes to leave him alone, but I am non-negotiable, everybody knows that.

When we're done, I leave him in front of the TV and go to my office to read. At noon, I cook cabbage soup and grill some fish and vegetables. It was last fall when the kids got me to set the grill up on the patio. I protested, worrying about the dirt and grease, but it works great. I can now grill eggplant and zucchini all winter long, flipping them and then stepping inside to watch the fire.

I do the laundry, hanging the clothes outside in the sun. Nobody does that in this neighbourhood, not even in summer. I know when they do their laundry because of the detergent smell coming from the dryer. Thanks to Adam, I can hang my laundry directly from the patio.

We knew it was illegal to attach the clothesline to the Hydro pole. The technicians that come by to check on the electrical wires threatened to pull it down. Adam said they could do that; they show no mercy when branches of the maple tree touch the wires. Fortunately, they haven't touched my clothesline.

The twenty-first of April is Adam's birthday. He's turning fifty, an age which used to make him quake. Sara asked me what I would like for him, as I'm now the real beneficiary of everything that concerns her father. I tell her we would like tickets to the opera. Her father always wanted to be the kind of person who lives well and goes to the opera. Immigrants don't often hang out at the opera.

Adam told me one day that for his fiftieth birthday he would like to do something special, something really different, like climb Mount Kilimanjaro or drive the length of Route 66. Now, the only novelty I can offer him is an evening at the opera.

Sara called me to report that the only show on right now is Gounod's *Faust*, I tell her that's fine, and she says she'll get the tickets.

On Saturday, the twenty-first, it rains all day. Since our arrival here, there has been bad weather on Adam's birthday practically every single year. Either it rains or it snows or, at best, it's just overcast. In the morning, we stay in bed a long time, I with my book, Adam with his comic strip.

In the afternoon we go to Costco. I don't like this store, but its prices are unbeatable for the Opera cake we like for our birthdays, Liberty yogurt, and Danish Blue cheese.

When we head out, I tell Adam we're going to the place with the best value for our money. He does not laugh. He has completely forgotten this old joke.

In the good old days, he honestly believed in getting the best value for his money at Costco, and he could never understand why I would tease him about it. One day, I explained.

"When immigrants start talking like this, they feel they've reached all their goals. They've finally made it."

I kept going. When an immigrant lands in this holy land of prosperity, he watches enviously as his old compatriots emerge from these warehouses pushing one of those space-ship-like carts loaded with goods. He cannot afford the annual membership fee and he especially cannot afford to throw away half of what he might buy. Buying at Costco represents not only prosperity but also a willingness to squander money. If you're not wasting money, in this country, you're not a good citizen.

We used to go to Costco from time to time just to use our card. Neglecting to renew our membership gave Adam the chill of dissidence. Failing to show off our Costco products as we carried them from the driveway to our front door was nothing short of rebellion.

I took advantage of those expeditions to renew my supplies of olive oil, canned peas and tomatoes, jars of dill pickles and roasted red peppers, detergent, almonds, raisins, and black socks for Adam. It had taken me some time – and some detailed calculations – to figure out which items really were less expensive here than at the Arabs or the Greeks.

That's why we would maliciously tell each other, "It's the best value for our money," whenever we headed out to Costco.

This morning, in silence, I help Adam get into the car.

Despite the rain and the early hour, customers are trampling one another. The filled carts collide in the jammed aisles. The traffic is even heavier around the tables where people can taste new products or items close to their expiry dates. People crowd around the frozen products, the aisles with grilled sausages, cheese, bread, wine, and beer. Everyone is hungry. By the time they've paid for their purchases, people have done their best to leave the place with a full stomach.

I get Adam behind me and dodge recklessly in and out of the crowd. I put an Opera cake into my cart, his favourite, a packet of pork chops that will last us two months, four jars of yogurt, two bottles of wine for unexpected visitors, salmon – $15 per kilo is a very good price – almond-stuffed olives, and Danish Blue cheese. That's all. This the last time I will set foot in this place.

I have to celebrate this decision. I offer Adam his last meal at Costco, saying, "We have to pay our tribute to America."

Adam says yes without knowing what he is approving. He has forgotten our teasing. I tell him to sit down at one of the tables while I go up to the counter for hot dogs and Coca-Cola. He avoids the eyes of a fat child at the next table.

We stop at the IGA on the way home. Tomorrow we will have some guests for his birthday, and I want to avoid having to go out in the morning just for a baguette, so I want to buy the kind of bread that stays crusty till the next day.

I suggest Adam take a nap. He says he prefers to watch TV. I don't understand how it can be that things that used to tire him out have no effect on him nowadays. As for me, a visit to the supermarket still takes a year off my life.

I go to the bedroom, draw the curtains, and get into bed. Fatigue crushes me when I remember that I still have to do the cleaning and most of the cooking. Maybe I should try the new practice of inviting people to a restaurant and getting them to pay for their own meal. Adam used to disapprove of imposing such an expense on our friends. They should at least get a free meal out of it when they bring a present.

It's six o'clock when I get started. Adam is watching a documentary on black caimans. He watches wide-eyed as scientists catch a huge specimen, load it onto a boat, carry it ashore and measure it. It's a huge female, about three metres long. The narrator says it's unusual for a female to exceed two-and-a-half metres, while males can reach four. They name her The Countess, a real matriarch. Despite her age, she can still reproduce. After tagging her, they follow her for a while during the feeding period before she lays her eggs.

I'm going to serve our guests a cream of pea soup, and I'll ask Michael to help out with the grill. I've set my heart on barbecued sausages and pork. There will be leeks with olives, as an accompaniment, and fried mushrooms with garlic and parsley. I'll also have potatoes and roasted peppers with vinegar and garlic. We'll end the evening singing, "Happy Birthday, dear Adam," around the Opera cake.

I cook until nine o'clock. Adam has settled in at the big table with his drawing book and his pencils. He's in a good mood, and he puts a lot of energy into practising his handwriting. He copies a whole paragraph in French to improve his skill with his left hand.

The phone rings a few times while I'm busy in the kitchen. I would like Adam to pick up, but he can't manage that yet. Old friends are calling to wish him happy birthday. Adam is reluctant to take the phone and talk to them, but he has no choice. Before putting the phone to his ear, he interrogates me with his eyes about what he should do. I cover the phone with my hand and whisper, "Just say thank you."

So this is what he does. At the other end, people can't even finish their sentence before he thanks them.

When I'm done, I sit on the couch. Adam is already comfortable, switching between two movies. On Télé-Québec, there's a Hitchcock movie – *Marnie,* I think – and on Astral, a movie in which Tom Cruise plays a serial killer. Adam stays on each channel just as long as there's action. He clearly prefers the one with Tom Cruise, but only while Cruise is punching people out.

At this level, Adam's instincts are still very male. He still loves tough guys who hit each other and cars that crash into one another.

I wake up at six o'clock on Sunday morning and look out the window, as usual. There's a huge black skunk in the backyard, with a white V all the way down its back. It's digging small holes in the ground, probably looking for seeds. I open the window and start banging the wall to shoo it away, risking getting sprayed with its rubber-like odour. It does nothing other than shiver almost imperceptibly at every thud. I decide to let it do whatever it wants, as I've only succeeded in waking up Adam. He's the one who notices the snowflakes.

"You see," I say. "There's always bad weather for your birthday."

The guests start showing up at one o'clock. The women sit on the sofa and the men in the kitchen around the counter. I serve Adam a gin and tonic, his first one since his stroke. The others prefer whisky. I've already prepared some appetizers with cheese, anchovies, and pickles.

This is the most beautiful moment of every gathering: the first sips of alcohol, the first nibbles, the first exchanges.

Dora and Marta have brought flowers for Sara. I told them she and Michael got engaged during their cruise. The women analyze the small diamond that Michael ordered in New York and asked a jeweller here to set in white gold. They want to know all the details of where Michael proposed, if he knelt down like a knight, if he was romantic, if it was during the day or at night. Sara has never been much of a storyteller, and the attention embarrasses her.

The evening they came to share the news, I passed over the event as discreetly as I could, unable to simulate an enthusiasm I did not feel. Sara and Michael have known each other since high school, they went to the same university, and they moved in together four years ago. This engagement brings nothing new; they were already a couple.

For our evening at the opera, I have to go downstairs to the storage area for the big box on which I have written: *May be useful.* In this I've packed away a few all-purpose suits that could serve a variety of occasions, ranging from weddings to funerals. Why not for the opera?

I choose light grey pants from one suit and a black wool jacket from another. I add a light mauve shirt and a red and black silk tie. Adam looks gorgeous.

For myself, I go for a beige linen dress that may be a bit too sporty, but it goes well with my black silk blazer with the velvet collar and cuffs. I pin on the Swarovski brooch, which was a gift from Sara for my forty-fifth birthday. After a minute, I complete the set with my Swarovski earrings, bracelet, and ring.

While we're lining up to enter the concert hall, I get confirmation that we go well together. Adam and I draw all the attention of the people around us. Just as everything in opera is based on make-believe, I enjoy these few moments of looking like an ordinary, healthy couple.

I don't like Gounod, but Adam is listening closely. From time to time, his eyes move to the conductor, whose head is caught in the floodlights. On stage, Mephistopheles is the character who interests him most. Adam follows him intently, I imagine because of his long black trench coat and his white makeup. The program says Alexander Vinogradov is the discovery of the season in the role, but I'm no expert. Even with his damaged brain, Adam may have a better idea of how good he is. I focus instead on the set, which is built out of large grey blocks that suggest a tomb, even when the action moves on to a banquet in the countryside.

At the first intermission, I take Adam out to the lobby for a drink. I want a beer, but I point to the wrong bottle. I thought I was getting a Heineken, but find myself with a huge glass of champagne instead, and I hate champagne. Adam tries it, uncertain.

He's forgotten what champagne tastes like. I realize we had some sparkling wine for his birthday.

"It's champagne, Adam," I tell him cheerfully, making the best of it. "For your birthday. Happy birthday, Adam."

He sips a small mouthful with satisfaction. He seems to like it more than the first time, and I pretend to like it, too.

My gloom intensifies with the misogyny in the third act. Mephistopheles says, "A woman should not trespass the door of her house without a ring on her finger." He condemns Marguerite to eternal damnation and humiliates her for her love affair with Faust.

During the second intermission, Adam and I go back out to the lobby, and this time I just watch people at the bar who have forgotten their manners. I'm feeling light-headed and out of sorts. Adam's smiley face makes me even grumpier.

I share my indignation with Adam, but then I realize I didn't explain the plot, so he has no idea what's been happening on stage. I completely forgot that he's unable to read the text in two languages running on a screen above the stage.

I summarize the story for him briefly, enough for him to understand why I'm angry. Imagine, an old man who wants his youth back just so he can womanize. And at the end, it's Marguerite who goes crazy and pays for his fantasy.

"Is he that bad?"

"Who?"

"Faust?"

"It is not because of Faust. It's because of the Devil who makes him sign the pact."

"Then what happens isn't Faust's fault. Everything was going to be that way."

"Yeah, yeah. And Judas had to sell Jesus out. Your male way of taking responsibility."

Adam isn't angered by my outburst. He keeps on smiling and is eager to get back to his seat. His feet don't hurt as mine do. I have to go to the washroom. Adam doesn't need to go; he still has a steel bladder. I tell him to wait for me here.

When I get back, I see Adam from a distance, and he looks so normal with his old habit of standing with his hands behind his back. When I get closer, I see it's only the good hand that's behind his back; the stiff one is at his side.

The student demonstrations make it difficult for us to leave the Place des Arts parking lot and get out of downtown. I have to make several detours until I unexpectedly find myself on Côte-des-Neiges. I then have no choice but to follow the road down Mount Royal, past Ridgewood to Queen Mary.

Adam is wide awake, staring at the streetlights, the neon signs, the flickering lights over shop windows, the customers smoking outside bars. We're almost alone on the street at this late hour, and I feel overwhelmed by the solitude of these crowded places.

We have not been out much recently. Adam has seemed more ill-tempered than usual, and I wonder if this could be the reason.

This weekend, I decide we'll go to Quebec City. The idea is thrilling at first, but the prospect of driving all that way makes me nervous. When we used to travel, it was Adam who drove while I listened to the radio with my bare feet up against the windshield.

I start packing on Friday evening. I even pack our toothbrushes, though I know we'll need them in the morning. After breakfast, I have nothing to do except slip our pyjamas and slippers into the bag.

It's mild outdoors, in spite of the wind that came up after mid-night and is now gusting powerfully as we leave the city. Adam looks happy in the passenger seat. After Trois-Rivières, he draws my attention to a huge flock of snowgeese resting on a lake beside the highway.

Half way, we stop for gas and coffee – and to give me a break. I've never been a good driver, and the long trip tires me.

Once we get to Quebec City, I follow our GPS, which leads me straight to the Clarendon Hotel. We were here once before, to cele-brate when Adam finished his MBA and found his first job as a proj-ect manager for an aerospace company. He was happy, but mostly proud about this, and glad to leave engineering for a new career. What with foreclosures and the manufacturing sector moving to Asia and Latin America, he figured the engineering field was finished in Canada. From now on, it would be a new world of speculation, management, and research. He pretended to be upset about the fact that his new job was resulting in his losing his engineering skills. What was the real job of a project manager? Simply put, to speak on the phone and check-in to hotels. It was a funny kind of job, really.

He worked at that for the last few years before his stroke, and he didn't enjoy the job at all.

He had no worries when we first came to the Clarendon Hotel. Sara had been accepted into dental school, we had paid off half our mortgage, and we had no other debts.

I still remember the rage I felt when I saw the $250 item on Adam's credit card bill. I told him it was criminal to pay so much for a bed. He answered that we deserved it every bit as much as the actors in those stupid ads for beauty products.

Today I'm paying $300, plus $28 for parking.

Our room is on the sixth floor, with a small living area and a double bathroom. Once I've hung our clothes up in the closet and put the toiletries on the glass shelf above the sink, I ask Adam if he wants to get some rest. He says yes. We take off our pants and socks and go to bed.

The hotel is very quiet, except from time to time, when we hear the elevator stopping at our floor.

We get up at four o'clock, feeling hungry. I help Adam get dressed, and we go for a walk around the Old Port. The wind gusts are strong and the light dazzling. Some of the tourists are in shirt-sleeves, but it's just for show. Their teeth are chattering.

In the Old Port, we look at a few shops and stop for coffee and cake. Adam has a lot of trouble climbing the stairs by the Château Frontenac. I have to sit him down on a bench to catch his breath.

We watch the river and the city of Lévis for a long time, on the far side of the St. Lawrence. I ask Adam if he wants to take the ferry just for the pleasure of being on the river, but he says he feels tired.

At six, we set off for the Crêperie Bretonne, our usual stop for supper. A rancid odour hits me at the door, instead of the sweet smell of caramel I remember from previous visits. We order one crêpe with bacon and another with maple syrup for dessert. We both love crêpes, but I rarely cook them because of the smell.

Back in our room, Adam crashes with fatigue. I have a bath, taking my time soaking in the bathtub. When I get back into the living room, Adam is in his pyjamas, watching TV. I don't insist he take his bath. His body has learned how to conserve its energy. He doesn't sweat a lot these days.

I buy a movie for us to watch, *The Artist*, which has just won the Oscar for best actor. This will increase our bill by $14. Adam falls asleep after just a few minutes; he no longer understands movies. When I think how much he used to love them.

In the morning, we're among the first in the restaurant. What we enjoy more than anything on our trips is a hotel breakfast. The big hall is already filled with a group of high school students chaperoned by some adults, probably their teachers. They must come from outside of Quebec, for they speak only English.

I tell Adam I find it strange that the school – or the parents – pay for such an expensive hotel for their children's trip to Quebec.

He does not understand what is strange about it. He has never had much money sense. He never found anything that pleased him expensive. He has always had a taste for luxury. Saving money and talking about the price of things has always displeased him. He used to pay without quibble for everything he wanted, and he wanted many things – postcards, souvenirs, sweets. When we were first married, we argued about this a lot, as I'm thrifty by nature. I was raised to believe that women should be thrifty. For the last few years before his stroke, though, I stopped checking Adam's bills. Mostly, I stopped reproaching him for buying me expensive gifts.

Adam eats with gusto. Maybe he recovers some part of his memory when he's faced with sausages, omelets, grilled bacon, cheese, croissants, pastries, little boxes of strawberries or blueberries, bottles of orange juice, apple juice, grapefruit juice, cartons of milk, and containers of yogurt. The colours, the odours, and the elegance of it all excite him. He gobbles up everything I put on his plate and asks for more. I agree and go back to the buffet with him in order to avoid any unpleasant accidents.

I allow him to help himself, and he arranges his food on his plate painstakingly with his good hand. He sets the plate carefully on the counter, grabs the spoon, taking more than he can possibly eat, then pushes his plate further along the counter. I tell him not to be in a hurry, he can come back for more

When we're full, we linger over our espresso in front of the large picture windows that overlook the street. Around us, the high school students are noisy, but their talk doesn't disturb us at all.

We go back to our room and decide to stay a bit longer. It's too cold for a walk, in spite of the bright sun. According to the weather forecast, the temperature dropped considerably overnight.

We loll around in bed all morning under the duvet. I read while Adam switches channels. He can't find a wildlife documentary and settles for the news, which shows crowds of students in the streets of Montreal. This is the eleventh week of the student strike.

Adam asks me what they want. I explain that they refuse to accept the government's hike in tuition fees. He asks me again if the hike is a good or bad thing. I tell him that school is like Costco; you get what you pay for. On the other hand, we ourselves have greatly benefitted from low tuition fees. If they were higher, no immigrant would ever be able to afford to get a diploma or train for a new career. Immigrants are the ones who should really be marching in the streets.

By eleven o'clock, I have the bags packed. Adam helps me out by putting the toiletries and the slippers by the suitcase.

While I'm checking out, the valet gets our car out of the garage and parks it at the door to the hotel. I give him a $5 bill.

Behind the wheel, I start laughing. Adam asks me why.

"Because of the tip I gave him," I say. "There's a first time for everything."

Close to the highway ramp, I change my mind about heading back to Montreal. "We'll do a little tour of the Île d'Orléans to check on our duck farm," I tell Adam.

He doesn't understand. He doesn't remember that we once planned to go into the duck confit business.

The wind is so strong on the island that I have to hold onto the wheel with both hands. There are only a few pedestrians, and their cheeks are purple with cold. It's less windy on the south shore, the sunny side with the farms and the orchards.

Every time we went to Charlevoix, we stopped here for a bottle of ice wine and a jar of duck pâté. One day, we saw a For Sale sign at a duck farm that got Adam very excited, and, all the way home, he talked about going into business. We'd go back to the land. We had to come here, to an island in the St. Lawrence, where the first settlers arrived four hundred years ago, the water their best defence against attack. Our Quebec roots were here, where the first log cabins and churches had burned to the ground and were buried under new buildings. I teased him about reconnecting with the ancient Gauls and betraying his Dace heritage and *mazare, brinza, viezure, varza*. My skepticism about his farming skills fell on deaf ears. He wanted to rebuild this country on a new foundation. "What foundation?" I asked him. He didn't quite know, but the dream lasted.

I ask if he would like me to stop somewhere and go for a walk. He says it's too cold.

I stop anyway, though, in front of Felix Leclerc's house, where we always used to stop. Adam looks at every picture on the walls while I read some lines of poetry that have been carved into the wood of the tables. We're the only visitors in the huge hall, which serves as a museum and occasionally as a venue for literary events. The young woman at the front desk greets us and then goes back to her reading.

I always check my email before leaving for school. This morning, there's a message from Dora, no subject. I hesitate before opening it; at this hour I don't have time to read the jokes and the miracle diets I always get from her. I'm early this morning, though, so I open the message before trashing it.

She writes that Virgil, her husband, had a serious road accident yesterday at 4.30 p.m. and is in hospital. There are lots of spelling mistakes in her message. At the end she says that all those who want to see him alive for the last time can do so this morning at Sacré-Cœur Hospital, on the fifth floor.

The telephone rings. Marta. She asks me if I want to go with her to the hospital. I tell her to ask Dora first, in case she isn't able to drive. She says she's already talked to Dora, and she needs to go in her own car so she can stop at the Police station afterwards to pick up Virgil's coat and keys. I decline her offer, too, because I'll have to go on to school.

It's been raining since dawn. I stay in front of the window for a few long minutes before going to the bathroom. Adam watches me anxiously; there are rarely any phone calls at this hour. If there's one thing that worries him more than anything, it's a disruption in our routine. I can't decide whether to let him know what's really happening, but his wary eyes make me realize that not letting him know would scare the shit out of him.

"Dora's husband Virgil had a motorcycle accident yesterday.

94

He's in hospital. I have to go and see him. It sounds as though he's been badly injured."

"Will he die?"

"I don't know, Adam. He could also get well. There are a lot of people who get into bad accidents and survive."

Adam bows his head. My reaction surprises him. He must be wondering why his question makes me so angry, when I normally remain calm, no matter what.

I have no time and I'm in no mood to set things straight. I rush into the bathroom and get dressed in the same clothes as yesterday, as I have no time to think of anything else. Before leaving the house, I explain to Adam one more time:

"I'm going to the hospital to see Dora's husband, who had a motorcycle accident. Then I will go straight to school. If I don't get home on time this afternoon, I'll be at Dora's place or at the hospital. I'll try to call you. Please, pick up the phone just this time. If it isn't me, you can just hang up. Ok?

Adam nods his head, but I know he will not touch the phone.

The traffic is already heavy all the way to the Lachapelle Bridge, where one lane is closed for road work. I mumble that all these people are going to see Virgil. This is what Adam and I used to say whenever we were caught in traffic, that everyone was heading the same place we were.

The hospital is not far from our house, but it takes me more than half an hour to get there.

In the corridor, the smell of bad news hits me in the face. This is the way I felt the day I came here with Adam, who was unconscious, and the feeling lasted the whole time he was hospitalized. The bacterium of unhappiness is etched deeply into these walls.

I am among the last to arrive on the fifth floor. A dozen others are crowding close to the door, anxiously asking for information.

Marta repeats the same thing to each new arrival, like a robot: "Tell me it isn't true."

We are waiting for the latest news from Dora, who is now with her daughter Nelly beside Virgil's bed. We send Eugene over to them, and he comes back with Dora. She tells us that Virgil had head surgery overnight in spite of the fact that the doctors were almost certain he could not be saved. His brain was flooded with blood and had ceased all of its activities except for hearing. The motorcycle fell with all its weight on his head, crushing it like a watermelon. She warns us that what we were going to see is not her husband any more, but a machine working for his body.

Cornelia, who is a nurse, advises her to ask for another tomography.

Some of the women are unsure if they can bear to see Virgil this way.

He's in the recovery room, where small areas are sectioned off with blue sheets fixed on clotheslines. Behind these sheets we can hear the heavy breath of machines.

When I go in with Marta, what I see is an old man with his mouth wide open and his eyes staring at the ceiling. An old woman next to the bed is holding his hand. It doesn't look as though he's still alive.

Virgil is lying naked under a white sheet. His head looks like a huge distorted cannonball, with a few bruises and scratches on his right cheek. The surgeons had cut out a hole in the right side of his cranium to reduce the internal pressure, but the pooled blood in his brain mixed with grey matter started gushing out, and there was nothing else to do than stitch his head back together and wrap it up in this disgraceful turban. His belly seems huge in comparison to his feet, which are as dainty as those of a ballerina in the elastic socks the nurse has put on to help his circulation.

Nelly is on the other side of the bed. She rubs her father's arm and whispers something in his ear. One of the machines shows a little rise in activity, but after a brief moment it falls back to tedium.

Out in the corridor, Marta starts sobbing. We're all thinking the same thing – it's impossible that that pile of flesh will come back to life.

The doctor is coming by at 9 a.m., and at that point the family will decide if they're going to unplug Virgil.

I can stay no longer, as I didn't call in sick. Marta can't take the day off either. Cornelia, Eugene and his wife will stay on, since Dora has no family here other than Nelly.

Outside, the rain has eased up a bit, but I don't have an umbrella and get soaked before I get to my car on the far side of the parking lot.

I can't pull myself together to teach. I tell the students I have a friend in hospital teetering between life and death, and that I'm in no shape to hold a class. I ask them to read a chapter from their mandatory reading: *The Road to Chlifa*.

The girls put their hands over their mouths when I tell them the news. Why is it that women cover their lips when they're surprised, afraid, or in shock? Is it to prevent themselves from crying out, yelling, or speaking? Young as they are, my female students have the same instincts as grown women.

The kids are compassionate and do as I ask. They're certainly happy with this unexpected change in their routine, which means there'll be no boring grammar exercises today. Abla, Loïc, and Krystel come to tell me that they understand my distress, for they've already been through something similar when they lost an uncle, a grandmother, and a cousin. They even express their condolences.

They imitate adults so well.

I do the same thing in the next class. The students learn the news while they're changing rooms, and the ones coming in surround my desk to ask if my friend is still alive. I tell them I don't know anything yet. They read silently for a bit, then start whispering. I leave them be and turn my back on them, looking out the window. It's pouring now. The schoolyard is already green. Further away, on the soccer field, a young man is playing with his dog.

At noon, I check my email. Marta has just sent a group message to let us know that Virgil died at eleven o'clock. They started unplugging the machines at ten o'clock, but Virgil had already stopped fighting. He had practically been killed during the crash. The doctor's job was to comfort the family. They had done everything possible, knowing that Virgil's heart would never stand the shock. We all knew how sick he had been. He had had heart surgery twice, so we'd been sure he would be the first of us to die. Part of what shocks us about this is that it messes up our bets on his weak heart.

I go to see Suzanne, the secretary, to ask her to find a substitute for my afternoon classes, as I'm not able to work. I explain the situation to her, and her hand flies to her mouth – the very same gesture.

When I leave the school, I head straight to Dora's. Their house is on a street that runs parallel to ours.

Her living room is already packed with twenty people. Dora has stopped crying. They gave her a pill at the hospital, and now she looks dizzy, with the swollen cheeks and puffy eyes that come of a sleepless night.

The younger members of our group are doing well. They're shocked, of course, but death's a thrill for them. Not for us. We're scared, perhaps for the first time. Virgil's death is the dress rehearsal.

We can no longer really be newcomers if we're burying one of our own. We're becoming like other Canadians.

The most active among us is Silvia, a young woman in her thirties that I hardly know. Dora and Virgil apparently spent part of their summer vacation with Silvia and her husband. Now she's become a kind of master of ceremonies. She loves playing this role, which she does until she gets on our nerves, though we don't much care as long as she does the job.

First, she gets paper so we can put together a list of everything that has to be done for the funeral. She makes me the official scribe, since I'm the teacher.

We start with the food that has to be bought today, as everyone who comes to the vigil will have to be fed. It becomes clear that we're all going to hang around until Saturday, the day of the funeral. Silvia decides on some pastries from *Serano's*, the Greek pastry shop, and Virgil's favourite Spanish red wine.

Virgil's cousin Aline has found a bottle of rum in the basement. She gives us each a big glass, and we gulp it down, wishing the deceased peace to his soul. Tradition calls for us to spill a drop on the floor, but we don't do that. We know how obsessed Dora is about her house.

The rum perks us all up, and my pen starts gliding more easily across the paper, which I mark with arrows and numbers to show how many dishes, napkins, bottles of wine, salt sticks, spinach rolls, cheese pastries, and fancy cakes we're going to need.

We move on to Virgil's suit, shirt, socks, and shoes. Someone says that people are buried barefoot over here, as they consider the deceased won't be doing any walking. We're all outraged. The winters are too harsh to leave a body shoeless!

We now have to decide if we should follow the Orthodox tradition.

The men really don't care, but the women decide they want to – which is when things get a bit complicated. Virgil died without confession, with no candle, and no priest. That means we'll need *pomnets*, a kind of white handkerchief with a coin tucked in one corner and a candle in the other. We're going to need to prepare sixty of these, which will be lit by sixty men when the body is lowered into the grave. This way, we'll be sure Virgil will be able to find his way up to heaven; the coin will pay for his passage on the other side. Someone asks how we can be so sure the money will pay his way up and not down. Someone else answers that the way down is free.

We laugh for the first time.

Silvia is appalled to notice that we have not yet covered the mirrors in the house. We do this at once, and Aline takes it upon herself to hang a black scarf outside, over the front door, to indicate there's a dead body in the house.

Where does this custom come from? From the time of the Black Death?

At four o'clock, the wine and the spinach-and-cheese rolls arrive. Just in time, as we're starving by now. More people are coming, everybody choosing to take the day off to be here. They're all jealous of me, as I'm one of the last of his friends to have seen Virgil alive and well, for he and Dora dropped by on Saturday to take me for a walk. The group wants to know if he said something that suggested he knew he was going to die. No, there were no such signs, he just acted and talked as usual. They decide this was a sign.

At nine in the evening, the house is bursting with people. The lucky ones, who had a comfortable place to sit, won't budge for anything in the world, even if they could. Some people are sitting on the floor, the men in the middle of the living room, the women in the kitchen.

I'm still the scribe, wielding the pen at Silvia's command. She asks me to be alert, and write down everything I hear and everything I myself remember of the traditions we grew up with and carried across the ocean.

So, there is this boutique on Notre-Dame Street; we have to send someone there for candles. We'll need to change money for the sixty coins, and we mustn't forget white cotton and scissors for the *pomnets*. Very important: we have to buy either a small Orthodox cross or a tiny icon with any saint protector for the casket. From the men's corner, a voice pipes up to tell us we'd better put one of Virgil's models inside, one of the miniature planes and helicopters he made as a hobby.

This gives me an idea for what I can write in the condolence book at the funeral home. I jot it down quietly on a piece of paper and slip it into my pocket: Safe flight, Virgil.

Dora is busy explaining what happened to each newcomer. She keeps saying it's driving her crazy that we left Virgil alone in a refrigerated box at the morgue.

By midnight people start leaving the house. I suddenly remember Adam. I grab my bag, put on my shoes and leave without saying goodbye. So many people are lining up to kiss Dora, and I can't wait. I ask Marta to make my apologies for me.

The rain has stopped. I take a deep breath, hoping to smell flowers, but all I can smell is the wet earth and the snow. Winter may still make a comeback.

Adam is watching TV. When he hears the key in the door, he comes up the stairs to greet me. He doesn't really remember the reason I'm late. When I tell him, he asks me about the place this person occupied in our life. This remains Adam's greatest concern, to know exactly what our life consisted of. Was this Virgil important to us? Did we really like him? Are we really affected by his death?

I sit down with him on the sofa and explain that Virgil was our neighbour, that we spent the last ten years together, ever since we bought this house, that in summer they used to invite us to their pool, and that sometimes we went for walks together in the park.

He says nothing and bends his head. He needs time to figure this out before asking another question. I admire his prudence.

He finally asks if Dora and Virgil were happily married. I say they probably were. People are happily married when they can't imagine living alone any more.

I ask him if he ate, and he says yes. I then suggest we brush our teeth and go to bed. I'm exhausted.

The next day, we try to get back to normal, but it's impossible. By noon, we're all back in Dora's living room, sacrificing our bank of sick days and our holidays to hang around and listen to the same stories.

Immigration had, until now, spared us this kind of experience, but Virgil's death is adding a few new twists to our migrant existence. We learn that the corpse goes directly from the morgue to the funeral home with a stop en route for the embalming. We have to find a Catholic cemetery willing to accept the Orthodox, which is not the case in every neighbourhood. And we discovered there are catering services offered by countless companies that can spare us, the women, the job of cooking for well over a hundred people.

We know how to party, how to celebrate birthdays, marriages, and baptisms, but we don't know how to organize a funeral. We make mental notes, learning as we go.

It's a challenge to find a priest. Virgil was a non-believer and profoundly disliked our black-robed servants of God. We figure we have to care about doing things properly to save his soul.

It turns out that at a recent commemorative feast for the mother of a friend, he got talking with a young priest who charmed him not with his faith, but with his good humour. We decide to find out who this good shepherd is and from which of our seven churches. Nelly's future mother-in-law takes charge of this, shutting herself in Virgil's office to make phone calls. When she finally finds our good Samaritan, she comes out with the phone for everybody to hear the situation.

The priest has a baptism on Saturday, but he could do the funeral too, if we agree to postpone it by half an hour. We happily agree, relieved to be able to tick off another of the tasks on my list.

On Thursday evening, we start tailoring the *pomnets*. Somebody has bought the cotton and a pair of scissors that cut in a zigzag pattern. The women are all amazed at this, and we each try them out on a piece of fabric.

Five women sit in the living room making the sixty handkerchiefs. Two wrap twenty-five cent coins in one corner of the fabric, while three others attach the long yellow candle to the opposite corner. It's Lily, Eugene's wife, who knew of the religious store on Notre-Dame Street where they sell these particular candles handmade out of natural wax. When we go to church, we pay a dollar each for them without ever wondering where they came from.

We're as solemn as the Pythia presiding over a sacred ceremony. We enjoy the prestige we have in the eyes of the mourners. No one dares disturb us. New arrivals enquire discreetly what we're doing, and we're proud to explain. People tell funny stories about funerals they went to as children in their villages and their neighbourhoods.

For the *pomnets* we've decided to follow the southern tradition, in spite of the fact that Virgil was born in Bucharest and did not give a damn about any of this. He belonged to an army family that was forbidden, by the Communist Party, from entering the church. He had a PhD in mathematics and another in aerospace, which Dora thought had something to do with his atheism. Maybe calculus and jumbo jets persuaded him there was no God.

This does not keep us from working on our *pomnets*.

Cornelia tells us we have a knot in the thread we're using for the coin and the candle, and that this is bad luck. We're halfway through and don't let this stop us. It would be just too much to undo and then redo so many pockets, and we've already had enough of this *merde*.

Virgil's co-workers tell us wonderful stories about how skilled he was, how good a friend, how kind a colleague. These are engineers from Bell Helicopter and also from Bombardier, where he used to work. Some people are here from the workshop, too, paying homage to their boss.

Dora listens in astonishment. The husband she knew was short-tempered and he never gave her any credit or accorded her any respect. He used to put her down in public, in front of their guests. We all knew this intolerant side of Virgil.

Virgil and I once argued about cats. I had mentioned that there were studies that suggest cats can carry a virus that makes their owners more aggressive. This is something I'd read in *Maclean's*, which Virgil abhorred from that day on. This virus survives in parts of the Third World but long ago was essentially eradicated in the West, except when it's passed on by a cat. A case in point is that of Colonel Russell Williams, who had been accused of sexually abusing and killing two women. It was when he got a cat, apparently, that his aggressiveness escalated.

We all look over at Virgil's cat, which has never budged from the front door, in spite of all the comings and goings. She just lies on the rug and stares at everyone who goes by. When one of the men tries to move her, she bites his foot. Dora hates this cat, and the feeling is mutual.

We spend five days together. Dora is looking much better and even starts joking about finding someone else. We feel we're not as welcome now, after days of keeping an eye on her, but we cannot stop ourselves from coming here. We can't get back to our lives until we see Virgil to his grave.

On Friday evening, the body is finally revealed in the funeral home. The embalmers did quite the job, we have to admit. There's no sign of the deformed creature we last saw, with purple skin and bruises, connected to transparent tubing like an Alien. He's a bit swollen, but we recognize his scowling face and black mood, poised to contradict every one of us. The left side of his head, which was shaved for surgery, is masked by white roses. The right side is darker.

The accident happened at a red light. He had just picked his motorbike up from the repair shop, where he'd had the front wheel fixed. The mechanic had warned him to make a few turns on a quiet street before going into traffic, in order to clear the oil from the tire. What he told the police is that Virgil was dismissive. "Look at my white hair," he would say. "You really think I still need you to tell me how to drive?"

So he rode straight into the traffic and the wheel started to lose its grip. Instead of slowing down, he accelerated, hoping to regain equilibrium. Fatal error. The motorcycle rose up on its back wheel, and Virgil went down, with 300 kilograms of hardware crashing on top of him.

Dora still has it in her to provide all these details.

At six o'clock in the evening, the priest comes to do the first Mass. Dora doesn't want to sit down, so five of us prop her up. From time to time she tries to push us away, for the room is already hot. We're so tired that the music makes us sleepy. A few rows back, some of the women start sobbing. These are more distant acquaintances who have just learned the news.

After half an hour we can finally go downstairs into a large dining room to eat and have coffee. We greatly appreciate the new items some of our friends have brought; after four days, we've had enough of Serano's pastries. We're happy to feast on taramasalata, oysters with cream cheese, pita bread with hummus, and sesame biscuits.

We're fed up seeing the same faces and hearing the same stories.

By nine o'clock, silence has fallen on the lounge. People sneak a look at their watches. We're all impatient for the funeral home to close its doors.

For some time now, Dora has been standing next to the casket. It looks as though she's whispering something in Virgil's ear.

This evening, I brought Adam with me. Now that we're all eager to leave this place, people look at him more often and with greater interest. He doesn't raise his eyes. At one point, he whispers in my ear that all these people look very old.

He's right. We've all become old, all of a sudden.

Do they think Adam is the one who should be lying over there?

I look at them whenever they stare too insistently at Adam. If there is someone above us who decides these things, he figured Adam was worthy of hanging around a bit longer. I'm determined to support this decision.

At ten o'clock sharp, I take Adam's hand and quietly ask him to get up. I think he's understood my contempt. Before we leave the room, he lifts his head and greets the group joyfully.

I don't bring Adam with me to the cemetery. I know it will be long and his leg won't be up to it.

The priest holds the farewell Mass in the funeral parlour, and I find it particularly beautiful. This is the first time I have listened to it so closely. The young priest has a wonderful voice, which really makes up for all these centuries-old Byzantine songs. People are crowding around to listen and gaze at the casket. There are newcomers who are still able to sob. We of the old guard are as silent as fish.

My God, Virgil was able to gather all these people together. Or is this an attempt to reassure ourselves that we're not just immigrants any more? We're starting to belong in this country.

Dora insists that the cortège take a detour to her street on its way to the cemetery. She wants to stop in front of the house for a few minutes to let Virgil have a last look. He bought this house ten years ago, an old building like all the others in the neighbourhood, and renovated it from top to bottom. He changed the wooden flooring, knocked down walls, changed all the doors, widened the living room, added a glassed-in porch, dug a pool, and planted a hedge that he used to prune meticulously.

The house is now ready for summer. The pool is painted, the grass is manicured, the dandelions have been uprooted. In a corner of the backyard he installed a gazebo because of the mosquitoes that proliferated in the hedge.

The cortège is blocking the street, even though we organized ourselves in such a way as to use as few cars as possible. The undertakers take the casket half way out of the hearse, but they refuse to open it. We get out, group ourselves around Dora and the casket and look at the two maple trees and the flower-beds for a few minutes. The front door is wide open, and the cat is lying on the threshold.

The cemetery looks creepy, just a strip of land between two streets in western Laval.

The priest holds a brief farewell Mass and asks the men to light their *pomnets*. Gusts of wind blow the candles out, and the men are so busy keeping them alight that they can hardly watch the casket being lowered into the grave.

We go back to the funeral parlour for the last feast. Nelly is not happy about the catering, finding the decorations ugly and the sandwiches ordinary.

We're shunted over to the tables. Marta was in charge of the *coliva* – the funeral cake we make out of boiled wheat seeds and nuts. She prepared ten trays, and there's none left over, for we all take some home in the plastic cups that have been set out for this purpose.

I get home by four in the afternoon to find Adam sunbathing on the patio. I had told him to take advantage of this wonderful day and he did. It's very hot, but there's supposed to be a heavy storm later and possibly some icy rain overnight.

I bring the plastic cup of *coliva* and a fork outside to him, but he puts it aside after one taste, saying it isn't sweet enough. I tell him that there are a lot of nuts in it though, and it smells good because of the cinnamon. He replies that he likes it sweeter.

I assure him I'm taking note.

I'm dozing in the living room on the sofa when the telephone rings. I wonder who it could be and consider letting whoever it is leave a message, but I decide to take the call.

It's Peter, calling from his house. He says he'd like to see me and talk.

"What do you want to talk about, Peter?" I ask, in a temper. It isn't twenty years ago. Can't he get that?

I want to hang up. I don't want to talk. But I cannot abandon him. I have a religious fear of doing wrong.

There's a long silence before he speaks again.

"We've decided to get a divorce. Lara has gone to a women's centre for a few days while I get my things out of here."

"It may be for the best."

My God. Why do I talk to him like this?

I don't know, but I can't pretend to feel compassion or any other good feeling. Peter has finally figured out that he should have left Lara a long time ago. Why would I comfort him for such an overdue decision?

He decides to leave me alone. He doesn't know what more to say.

The tone of my voice has alerted Adam. Peter's calls have a destabilizing effect on him, too. I catch his frightened gaze and see he's no longer watching TV. He must have heard Peter's name. Does it jog his memory? Does he remember this man?

"It was Peter," I tell him. "Lara's husband. They came over in the winter."

He doesn't remember, but asks, "What does he want?"

"I couldn't understand. There was a lot of interference on the line."

Adam understands this explanation; he gets it quite often.

Sometimes he draws what has alarmed him. One day, he drew tunnels with cars that were trailing white clouds like the speech bubbles that come out of the mouths of comic strip characters. He told me this was traffic on the telephone wires.

This time he draws two people at a table, a man and a woman, apparently on a restaurant terrace. There are some passersby, too, and some sort of bus with two sticks on top attached to hanging wires. Probably a trolleybus.

I was twenty-six years old when I got the call that every woman fears.

Instead of dreading that they may be cheated on, what women really dread is their own reaction when they find out. Is there any comfort in getting the news from a close friend? Some people say there is, especially when the messenger is also the cuckold.

When Peter called to tell me that Adam was having an affair with his wife, I asked him if he was in his right mind. I took advantage of this short moment of disbelief to remain polite, before my brain started the long process of digesting the news.

When this happens between friends, there are lots of questions you don't have to ask, such as when and where the affair started. It was all there, right under our noses, at our weekend get-togethers, our outings, our daily conversations, the visits we missed, the mention of this excuse and that one. We just had to scratch the surface a little to know what certain looks, smiles, pretences, and insinuations actually meant.

Peter still made me smile with his Russian accent. The more distressed he was, the more hilarious he sounded. I even wondered if he was doing it on purpose to spare me. He wasn't. He was too upset to care about my feelings. He'd been here a long time, but he just couldn't shake his accent, and when he was nervous, he spoke terrible Romanian. I think he never really put his mind to learning the language properly; he lived in the hope of one day returning to

Moscow. What stopped him was Russia's instability since the fall of Communism — that and its ex-KGB leaders. After he got his PhD, he worked as a university professor in Bucharest; Lara worked for a foreign company. There were in-laws and their connections, a big flat in a pricey neighbourhood, twin girls, and a bunch of new friends — Adam and I among them. He was popular, too, as fifty years of Communism had isolated Romania so much that foreigners were welcomed, even Russians. We hated Russia but never the Russian people.

Peter knew he would never go back to live in Russia, even after he found out Lara was cheating on him, but her betrayal ruined his adoptive country for him. He felt like an outsider with no family connections and no support. He turned Lara's treachery into a general betrayal. He was paranoid people were plotting against him, and he was afraid of being humiliated in public settings. He suspected his colleagues of shunning him and his friends of talking behind his back.

I pitied him, but his irrational distress also made me very uncomfortable.

That afternoon, I agreed to go out with him and have a coffee. He was insistent that we see each other face to face, discuss the situation, and figure out a strategy. We would meet at a coffee-house or a restaurant, ideally, so we could avoid minefields that would hurt our feelings even more. Was it at our place or at theirs that Adam and Lara had been sleeping together?

We chose a small café near the university. It didn't seem to dawn on him that some of his students might see him in such distress.

It was the end of June, so warm and pleasant, but the joy of the young just added to our misery. Our partners' disloyalty robbed us of our youth. Our loss of confidence made us skeptical and suspicious.

I was disappointed, and yes, wounded, but Peter's torment made me aware of my responsibilities. Why does a man still take his wife's betrayal so hard? Is adultery such a recent invention that men have not had time to figure out how to deal with it? Let's face it; a woman can cheat on her husband, too. How could I say any of this to Peter, who was weeping and attracting a lot of attention to us?

If it hadn't been such a ridiculous situation, I would have tried to comfort him. What did he want to hear? What does one say to a cuckold? That his wife would come back to him? That it wouldn't last? That the other man, the lover, deserved no consideration?

Why do men and women look for adventure outside of marriage? Stupid as it may seem, this is the key question, and there's no good answer. What is passion made of? What subtle mechanism shifts a double life into gear?

The reason I hadn't figured out what Adam was doing is that I had never asked myself if my husband would one day betray me.

We were young and still in love. We had a young daughter, good salaries, a nice downtown apartment. We were well off, compared to people we knew, and we had the support of watchful families and good friends. We had both had happy childhoods, and our youth spanned two regimes, which allowed us to make the transition from one to the other without significant trauma. Why go looking for catastrophe? I would have led this uneventful life until the end of the time, with no complaints. I wasn't looking for any extra excitement.

Peter was. He discovered his wife's affair because he needed that frisson. He needed an extreme situation, and he got one. Not me. I resented him for disrupting the course of my life. He should have known the affair couldn't go on. There were too many watchful eyes and they couldn't keep an affair hidden for long. They would have called it off to save their marriages.

Peter was not convinced. He was sure they would ask for a divorce and move in together. I told him that if it that were the case, they'd have done it sooner. If you don't leave your partner quickly, you're not going to leave at all, for the new relationship will start to feel like the first one, with the same kinds of predictability and the same kinds of demands, reproaches, and disputes.

I was ready to face both eventualities. If Adam wanted to leave me for another woman, there was nothing I could do about it. How could we keep on living together if he no longer loved me? And, if the affair was just a fling, why create a stir and destroy everything we had?

Peter was appalled by my reasoning. Was I made of stone?

I was almost ashamed of my own insensitivity. Unlike Peter, I was preoccupied by things that required my full attention. I was in the midst of my final exams, I had a mountain of papers to correct, a hundred school reports to write, and a graduation ceremony rehearsal to attend. After getting my diploma in teaching foreign languages, I was among the fortunate few who got a job at a very good high school in the centre of Bucharest. Challenges at my new workplace were counterbalanced by my pride in this accomplishment. My life wasn't easy with so many young people sapping my energy. When I ran into them in the halls, their young bodies stripped all vigour from me. I had to make a big effort to protect myself against the magnetism of their youth. Was I getting old?

I asked myself this question at twenty-six; I don't do that any more.

What could I say to comfort Peter?

I urged him not do anything for now. We had to act as though nothing had happened. Whether from fear or for some other reason, he agreed. I suspect he didn't feel ready to face a scandal. And this hesitation turned out to be his final verdict. He had already effectively decided to accept the situation as it was.

We decided that the best way of dealing with the shock was to avoid face-to-face meetings with Adam and Lara. We had to find ways of cancelling rendezvous plans and be sure not to plan any others.

When I left Peter, I went back to school to finish my day's work. My colleagues were in a good mood; the school year was nearly over. Marking so many exams was a big job, but we preferred that to our classes.

At day's end, we had got together in the staff room over a pot of coffee and a cake one colleague had brought. I laughed heartily at the bawdy jokes and talked about my holiday plans. I almost completely forgot Peter and his gloomy face.

It was only on the trolleybus, on my way home, that it all came back to me. Adam was cheating on me. He did not love me anymore. Our life together was a lie.

I saw myself as I was, sitting on the red plastic seat, broken, staring through dirty windows, my body shaken as we crossed trams rails and potholes. I looked old.

When I stood up at my stop, I met the eyes of a woman standing beside me and realized I had been crying.

As I drew near to our building, I tried to compose myself. I was sure I'd bump into Lara's mother, as I usually did.

I was right: there she was, sitting on a bench with some elderly neighbours. She was fond of me, and I liked her, too. I used to stop to chat with her for a few minutes before taking the elevator to our third floor apartment. She lived on the fourth floor, and Peter and Lara were on the seventh.

My God, I thought when I spotted her, how cunning of Adam and Lara to dodge the secret police of this place. They must be seeing each other somewhere else.

Lara's mother was retired, and she spent her days outdoors, at the entrance to the building. Other old ladies in the building were thought of as shrews, but we all liked Lara's mother. She was kind, her voice was soft, and she loved the kids she took care of.

I stopped, as usual, to chat with her.

However, a brief exchange of a few words was enough for me to understand she knew everything. A timidity in her eyes, her hesitation to touch my arm as she usually did, her impatient movements, and unnecessarily straightening the collar of her blouse all told me that nothing was as it had been.

She knew it, too. She was ashamed of acting as though nothing had happened. And my response had the effect of letting her know things were not the same from where I stood, either. I was not the same around her. And she could tell that I knew.

I moved away as fast as I could, pretending I had things to do.

How long had she known? Had she caught them together, in Peter's own bed? That was the most likely possibility, as she had a key to their apartment. And Lara? How could she continue carrying on an affair when her mother was aware of it?

Wicked old witch, I said to myself in the elevator, hitting the button to the third floor.

I was setting my bag down in our apartment when the phone rang. My heart jumped, as though a shotgun had gone off right beside me.

It was Adam. I knew it. Before leaving his job, he always called to ask if we needed anything. He had the car, so he did the errands, which was something I was very grateful for.

I tried to stop my hand from shaking and control my voice. I didn't want Adam to guess my new mental state – not until I knew what I really wanted. I told him to buy some eggs, milk, and apples. He asked if there were none left, as I had asked for the same things the day before. I said I wanted to make an apple pie.

After he hung up, I had to lean against the wall. This was not going to be easy.

I needed something to calm me down. I didn't know if I needed to drink water, or coffee, or pop a pill. How could I prevent the distress, the rage that had started to grip me? I was feeling the effects of the adrenalin that was pumping through my body to protect me from disaster. I followed the rapid course of the chemicals flooding in my veins, and yelled, "Not yet, not yet."

I had to be quick and figure out the gestures and the words that would allow me to play-act my usual self. I had to rehearse normality.

What did I usually say to Adam when he came home? Did I hug him, kiss him, take his coat, carry the shopping into the kitchen? What did I have to do that very afternoon in order not to betray myself, as I had undoubtedly betrayed myself with Lara's mother? Or was it only a person who already knew what was going who would notice a change?

The old woman must have been living for months with the terror of this confrontation. And that day, when she saw me, she understood the time had come for her to protect Lara. It was cruel of me to postpone the quarrel. She would have it in for me for that.

Adam had no clue about my new attitude. He didn't seem to realize that I didn't invite him to eat right away. Usually, the babysitter brought Sara over, and when I got home, I looked after her and prepared a snack for Adam. This afternoon, I'd asked the old lady who looked after her to keep her for a few more hours. She was used to this request when we went out for the evening; she was pleased to get paid overtime, so she never minded. Adam didn't even seem to realize Sara wasn't home yet.

I watched him while he ate. He told me about his day, as usual. I listened closely to see if there had been any change in his routine. Everything sounded so... so normal.

That day, like any other day, he hugged me when he was done and held me against him for a while to feel his sex getting hard. He bit my neck and touched my breasts.

He was still my husband.

Everything Peter had said was pure fantasy. Why had I not asked him for more details instead of believing this nonsense? He could be wrong and he could ruin my life for nothing.

It had been a long time since Adam's presence had got me so excited. I wanted to feel his touch and I wanted to see him. I was eager to listen to him talk, not in order to prove he was cheating on me, but in order to prove he still loved me. I wanted so much to be reassured that he was betraying me out of stupidity or because of a craving for novelty, not because I disgusted him, not because he'd had enough of me.

That evening, watching the news, I laid on the couch with him to feel his body. It was a long time since I had wanted to be intimate with him as much as I did then. His arm held my waist, and his fingers smoothed down my hair so he could watch TV over my head.

During a commercial break, he pulled down his pants, and we made love. I warned him that I was in my fertile period, and he said that was OK. Sara needed a little brother anyway.

He was definitely still my husband, body and soul.

The next day, I decided to forget what Peter had said, but it wasn't easy. I woke up with the terrible feeling that my body could no longer protect me from myself. The protective hormones had stopped rushing around inside me. Now it was the turn of the black knights of doubt, despair, and disbelief. I managed to pull my body to the bathroom as if it had suddenly become old and decrepit.

To save myself, I complained of a terrible headache. I just couldn't carry on making breakfast and getting Sara ready for the babysitter. Adam was not used to this new me, but no doubt he had friends who had warned him it would happen. Sooner or later, a wife stops being a goddess and turns into a shrew. Sooner or later, she starts feeling exploited. Is this what was happening?

Adam got on with all the chores without saying anything. He fed Sara, dressed her, and then left the apartment after checking to see if I was doing any better.

Later, when I was at work, Peter called me again. I had both feared this and wished for it. He could not stand the solitude, the silence. He was in pain, physically. He had a ghoulish need to talk and to understand. He asked if we could meet in the afternoon for coffee.

I agreed. The school where I worked was not far from the university. The trolleybus stop was at the corner, and the trip took five minutes.

This time, Peter had chosen the terrace of a small restaurant. He said the café where we had met the day before made him sick. He would always associate that place with the nausea he was feeling that day. He needed to eat something, too. When he got home after our meeting, he had pretended to have a stomachache and went straight to bed. He was unable to go through the motions of everyday life. He was less gifted than me at play-acting. He also feared his physical strength. What if he hit Lara in a moment of rage, or even killed her?

The ways in which the two sexes differ, when faced with adultery, is not in the state of their heart but in the power of their muscles. The difference between Peter and me was that he could relieve his anger with a few punches.

We ordered pork chops. Peter asked me if I wanted a glass of wine. In fact, it was not so much a suggestion as a command to keep him company. He didn't want to get drunk, just to anaesthetize his pain. I accepted a glass of red wine. After a short hesitation, Peter changed his mind and ordered vodka. He asked if I wanted to smoke. I had stopped when I got pregnant, but I accepted and took a cigarette.

The vodka had the effect Peter had counted on. His eyes filled with tears. He was watching me, waiting for something nice, unexpected, encouraging. His eyes were begging me to touch him, rub his hand, kiss him on the cheek. He desperately needed to be comforted, a few kind words to soothe his awful pain.

I told him I was sure Lara still loved him. This was what I wished to be told in turn. He did not reciprocate.

From that day on, the practice of play-acting our normal life at home carried on along with this daily rendezvous. Peter and I ate and had coffee together at lunchtime. We stopped talking about what had brought us together. I didn't ask for details, and he lacked the courage to say more. Did he have any photos, videos, tapes? Had he hired a private detective? What was it that tipped him off?

I did not want to know more. I accepted his revelation, as I had no choice, but I didn't want to hear anything further.

One day, I told Peter that his mother-in-law was certainly aware of the affair. He completely denied it. He was convinced the old woman would never give her consent to this horror. I did not insist. It surprised me, though, that Peter was able to discover his wife's betrayal but not to track down her accomplices.

What childish naïveté. Peter believed in his wife's vileness but not in her mother's. He did not understand the first thing about a mother's determination to protect her offspring.

As for me, I already knew I was right. For some time now, Lara's mother had not been in her usual spot at the front of the building when I came home. I was glad about this, as it would have been difficult for me to see her. I knew, though, that things would not stay this way.

One day, I had to face the situation I was preparing myself for.

I had just gotten home and had kicked off my shoes when the doorbell rang. My heart started beating like crazy. I knew without a doubt it was the old lady.

I opened the door.

There she was, with tears in her eyes, unable to utter a word.

My hands became suddenly cold. From that moment on, nothing in the world could make me doubt that my husband was having an affair. I doubly hated this woman for removing my last shred of hope.

"You should be ashamed of yourself!" I said, and then I slammed the door in her face.

The next day, I asked Peter if he had noticed any change in Lara's attitude. He said no. I couldn't trust him. He was no longer able to tell what was normal from what was not. I didn't tell him about the old woman's visit, but I was sure Lara had been warned. What was she doing at this very moment to protect herself against the fear of seeing her secret revealed in the cruel light of day?

At home, I was doing a good job of simulating normality. In the morning, I did not need to fake a headache. I woke up numbed by the passionate lovemaking of the night, for Adam's betrayal had stimulated a voracious sexual appetite in me. My desire was fed by my profound knowledge of his body, by the familiarity of his smell, his strength, his gushing sperm. Adam seemed unappeasable, too. I did not understand any of it; I just surrendered myself to my passion, my hunger for him, without knowing if I was experiencing the end of our relationship or a new start.

I got used to seeing Peter at lunchtime, and we prolonged our meetings more and more. We went well together. We sat in the sun on the terrace watching the pedestrians and the traffic on the boulevard.

This situation might have gone on like this for a long time if Adam had not happened to see us one day. He was crossing the boulevard in his car, heading to one of the branches of the company he worked for. Behind the mass of vehicles, passersby, and trolleybuses, he caught sight of us on the terrace with our plates and glasses of wine.

He could not stop because of the traffic and because there was nowhere to park, but I noticed a change in his attitude as soon as he came home that evening. A certain hesitation in his eyes and the tentativeness of his hug and his kiss warned me. He was acting the way Lara's mother had acted. I had already charted the psychology of guilt and easily recognized it in my husband.

He was afraid of accusing me of anything. He asked me the question as genuinely as he could: why was I meeting Peter on the terrace without mentioning it? Was it a pre-arranged rendezvous or a habit?

I told him I was seeing Peter from time to time to have coffee together.

Adam got it. Peter and I were either lovers or confidants. Either we were sleeping together or we were licking each other's wounds. Which one of these variants did he prefer? Which one was more difficult to bear? Which did he fear more?

I kept quiet. My hands were shaking, but I happened to be busy in the kitchen, preparing supper. The stirring of food on the stove and the chopping of onions and carrots justified my long silence. I avoided his eyes, his questions. I intentionally delayed my answers. I was torturing him.

I pretended to change the subject, asking him to bring me some canned tomatoes from the pantry. Adam obliged and was silent for a few minutes. I put his snack on the table and carried on with the supper preparations.

Sara was in the living room with her dolls. This was the difference: when Adam came home he dropped his bags and went in to play with her, to kiss her, to throw her in the air. During the day, he missed his daughter physically. This is what he once told me.

This time, he just kissed her and sent her off to play with her toys while he had his snack. He wanted to be alone with me to assuage his doubts.

He was swallowing pieces of salami and cheese with great difficulty. I served him a beer, and he was grateful. He pushed his plate away, barely eaten, and put his elbows on the table. He was focusing on the bottle. By the time he'd finished it, he asked me if Peter was well. I answered that he suspected that Lara was cheating on him with one of their friends.

He hesitated for a long time before asking me this question:

"And what do you think?"

"Anything is possible," I said. "But I think it's pathetic."

He stood up, saying that he was going to take a shower and go to bed, that he did not feel well. When he had gone, I went to comfort Sara, for in her own way, she too felt this was not a regular day for us.

I finished my supper and gave Sara her bath. Adam had come back to the living room. I let him sleep or rest without questioning him. I tried as much as possible to keep my own normality, even though I was not sure there was any normality, where I was living.

The next day, Peter called me at work to tell me when he could leave the university. I told him I had an important meeting with the principal and the staff, and it would be impossible for me to join him. He insisted. He said he was ready to take a day off and find a substitute to teach his class, if this was all right with me. He had to see me. He just couldn't go home without soothing his grief.

I told him it was impossible for us to go on like this, with secret meetings and vodka in the middle of the day. Nothing would ever change what we had learned. It was time for him to decide whether to forgive.

As for me, I was ready to give Adam a second chance.